I DIDN'T KNOW WHAT TO SAY, SO I JUST SAID THANKS

Stories

DAVID JOSEPH

©2023 By David Joseph
Published by Portal 6 Press
A number of stories in this collection have previously appeared elsewhere: "Fishing" in *The Fredericksburg Literary and Art Review*, "I Didn't Know What to Say, So I Just Said Thanks" in *Five South*, "A Real Man" (now titled "Travis") in *Wraparound South*, "Highway 5" in *Havik*, "The Clothes" in *Vessel*, and "The Last Time" (now titled "The Anniversary") in the *Munyori Literary Journal*.

All rights reserved. No part of this publication can be reproduced or transmitted in any form or by any means. This book is a work of fiction. Names, characters, locations, and events are the product of the author's imagination and any resemblance to persons, living or dead, events, or places is entirely coincidental.

Edited by Emma Moylan
Cover by Die Welle Design
ISBN 978-1-7359191-4-0

I DIDN'T KNOW WHAT TO SAY, SO I JUST SAID THANKS

ALSO BY DAVID JOSEPH

Fiction:

The Old Men Who Row Boats and Other Stories

Poetry:

The White Pigeon

For my wife, Karen, the incredible woman who has listened to my stories for more than twenty years and always encouraged me to write them down.

ACKNOWLEDGMENTS

I hadn't written fiction in nearly twenty years when I began writing short stories again in 2016. I always tried to keep writing, but I found myself attracted to other mediums. There were times when I wrote poetry and others when essays and op-eds captured my attention. But never fiction. Not as a writer.

Perhaps I was just too intimidated to take another crack at it. After all, I never stopped reading fiction. If anything, my love and admiration for Hemingway and Carver and Chekov had only grown over the years. And I had discovered new writers, with the prose of Haruki Murakami, Lucia Berlin, and Mario Vargas Llosa now swimming in my head as well. So, it was not for lack of inspiration that I had failed to craft any fiction. Only courage.

There were no plans for me to overcome it, but one day I found myself beginning to write a poem that called for a more prosaic voice, lines that called for me to stretch them out, and a narrative that was best suited to another form, a new form (or an old one) depending on how you look at it. Just like that, there I was, writing fiction again, after all these years. I was wholly unsure of what would become of those stories or even if they were any good, but they seemed to have, well … something. They had, at the very least, been born in an authentic place, and I did my best to honor that.

The first stories I wrote were set in Spain and Portugal, and a number of them were included in my first collection, *The Old Men Who Row Boats and Other Stories*.

The stories in this book are all set in the United States. They cover a lot of ground, traveling from the American South to California and the Mexican border. Through it all, the stories are uniquely, unapologetically, well … American. Black. White. Latino. Male. Female. Drunk. Sober. Happy. Sad. Old. And young. Yes, young. They are young in the way America is young—the characters searching, struggling, seeking, and trying to grow amidst all of the pain that comes from changing, the pain that comes from evolving. Whether the characters succeed is not easy to define, but they keep going, keep moving, keep trying.

Along the way, there were a number of people who kept me going. To my editor, Emma Moylan, thank you for always helping me work to search for the right words and for your guidance in helping me arrange them. Your knowledge and expertise were vital to making sure these stories were as close to perfect as they could be, that every i was dotted, and every t crossed. I relied on your skill to catch the things I failed to see, and you did. To my cover designer, Katarina, I am grateful for your efforts to design this beautiful cover in the spirit of the words that are inside it. To my layout editor, Walt, you simply make every page, every paragraph, every font, well ... look better.

Lastly, to my family, you are the source of both my stability and my inspiration. Along this solitary journey, one in which I poured all my emotions into the project, you always reminded me that everything would be OK, that everything was OK, more than OK, because I had the three of you. It is unimaginable to assess the immense value of this gift, and I can only say thank you, thank you, thank you.

TABLE OF CONTENTS

FISHING	1
I DIDN'T KNOW WHAT TO SAY, SO I JUST SAID THANKS	10
LOCALS	21
ORVILLE'S	32
SOUTHERN HOSPITALITY	60
HIGHWAY 5	99
THE BORDER	106
HENRY AND THE COWBOY	116
TRAVIS	127
FISH THAT LEAP	143
THE ANNIVERSARY	151
THE MILKMAN	156
ALL THAT REMAINED	171
THE RIVERBOAT CASINO	181
EVEN AFTER ALL THESE YEARS	196
I WOULDN'T HAVE KNOWN	215
THE CLOTHES	230
WIDOWERS	238
LEAVING TOWN	247
ABOUT THE AUTHOR	257

FISHING

It's hard to believe that I had refused to go fishing with my dad for years. I didn't just make up excuses. I didn't try to let him down easy. I just told him. I just told him straight out, straight to his face, and I broke his heart. My dad had a spirit that went on for days, but each time I refused to go fishing with him, I knew that I crushed it a little bit. It was harsh, but I was only seventeen. That's what boys do when they are seventeen. They push back. They stand their ground. Carve their own path. Try and prove that they are a man, that they are their own man, or damn close. And that's what I did. It's not like I didn't like going fishing with him. I did like fishing, and I liked fishing with my dad. But he loved it. He loved it more than any other activity in his life, and I knew that he felt this way. This made it simply impossible for me to wholeheartedly embrace it, at least if I was going to demonstrate the absolute individuality of my being. If I was going to differentiate myself from him, it was necessary to hold my ground, to exhibit some level of resistance. I know this sounds childish, and it was. It was childish and petty and hurtful, but it was only meant to be temporary. It was only meant to be imposed for a time. Then, after my strength had been asserted, we would spend many more hours together in the boat, casting out into the cold waters with the sun at our backs and the day just coming up and the fish unknowing of our formidable presence. I was still young, and I knew there were many more years to go fishing with him.

The winter was colder than expected, and the snow fell from the sky and covered our property. Although it looked beautiful, it was an illusion, a mirage, something that makes a Christmas Eve look nice on television but is little more than a hassle in reality. And, make no mistake, a blanket of white snow was a hassle, a burden. It was work, and the work began as soon as the morning was upon us and with it the realization that the driveway and walkway were concealed, kept from view below inches of snow that needed to be relocated in order for us to effectively begin the day.

Dad liked to complain about the weather more than anyone, but he also liked to prove that the elements were no match for him. Or perhaps a better way of saying it is that he liked to prove that the elements wouldn't get the best of him. He was in his fifties now, and he wasn't as young as he once was. But he liked to show me that he shouldn't be underestimated, that he was still powerful and resilient and able to complete physical tasks without the help of others. A blizzard gave him the opportunity to reestablish his presence and remind me of his air of invincibility like nothing else. So, while he complained about the weather, he also welcomed it, almost taunted it, and made it clear he would be the last man standing in it. This wasn't merely an immature act of a man trying to recapture his youth. This was my father holding on for dear life, clasping to the things that make a man feel most like a man—the gripping strength in his hands, the ability to endure beyond all reason, and the need to lift weight as a sign that his muscles weren't confined to the virility of youth, that they could sustain themselves over time, and that the world still had to take notice of him physically. All his wit and intellect and mental acuity meant nothing to him if he couldn't plunge his shovel into the wet snow, hoist it into the air, and toss it confidently to the side. He didn't just want to do it. He had to do it.

The winter snowfall had been minimal, and by February it seemed we might actually escape and emerge in the spring unscathed. But it was not to be, and we woke to find a snowfall unlike anything we had seen in a number of years. Schools were closed. Businesses let employees know they should work from home, and local government buildings shut down. But we were fine. It was warm inside, and we had plenty of food and supplies in the house. Although we were effectively snowed in, there was no reason to fight against it and no real benefit to all the work it would take to clear the snow. We were safe and warm, and it did look beautiful outside, particularly since we had nowhere to be or go.

But my dad didn't take on the elements for practical reasons. He took them on for psychological ones—his physical productivity being one of the keys to his psychological health. I sat there at the breakfast table while my mother slept, and he grabbed a cup of coffee and a small bite of food and peered out the window carefully. He was analyzing the situation, sizing up precisely what he was up against, and determining the best way to attack it. All this while the snow continued to fall at a steady rate. The sun was just coming up and it cast a warm glow across the white snow, giving the illusion the frigid temperatures would be palatable. Although shoveling snow was the last thing I wanted to do, I couldn't watch him go out there alone. He would never have asked me to help him, but this was the opposite of fishing. Here, I felt compelled to demonstrate that I was up to the challenge, that my arms were beginning to fill out, and that I could muscle the snow with every bit as much vigor as he approached the job. He certainly wasn't going to wait for me, so I grabbed my hat and gloves and put on my boots quickly and tossed my jacket over my pajamas to ensure I wasn't left behind even with sleep still in my eyes.

When he opened the door, a blast of cold air tunneled through the side door and seized our faces. The glare was bright, and we grabbed the handles of the shovels and began to dig our way out. I was working harder than usual in order to show my dad that I was his equal, that I was tougher than he thought, and that the lessons of his example hadn't been lost. He matched me with each plunge, lift, and toss, as if to remind me that he hadn't lost a thing. We didn't say a word. We were just two men, two generations of men, and something of a silent, mutual admiration society until I saw my dad stop. He stood up straight and looked around. I thought he was just admiring his work, as his head turned on a swivel and his eyes seemed to sharpen. Then he said he just needed to use the bathroom. He turned his back to me and walked inside the house. I let him know that was no problem, and I kept shoveling away with the cold air blasting my face and the sun ascending higher into the sky.

When my father went into the house, I began to work faster, more diligently, and with more urgency—not so much because he wasn't there, but rather because I hoped I might finish before he returned. What a display of strength and productivity it would be for him to return from the bathroom only to see the driveway cement now visible. This would be sure to impress him, force him to take notice, real notice, of my arrival. He would see that I could get the job done, that I could battle through, and that I was capable of working at a furious pace when life required it. There would be no mistaking my capacity when he returned. And so, I worked like crazy, attacking the snow with uncommon zeal, over and over and over, shoveling it aside and clearing the walk impressively. It wasn't long before I was finished, and I wondered why my dad hadn't returned. Was he not feeling well in the bathroom? Had he looked out the window and become intimidated upon seeing me conquering the elements? That seemed unlikely. Whatever the reason, I went into the house to find him.

When I opened the door, I was just about to kick off my boots when I saw his inert body lying on the floor. Somehow, I knew he was gone, that his soul was no longer there in the room, from the first moment I saw him. Still, I rushed to him, called 911, and worked feverishly in an attempt to revive him. Although I knew these efforts would amount to little, I continued without letting up. My mother ran into the room, knelt to the floor, and held my father's hand with tears streaming down her face.

When the paramedics arrived, they began where we left off before recognizing there was nothing left for them to do. They took great care to cover my father and remove him from our house as respectfully as possible. They walked out the front door with the gurney and wheeled my father's motionless body down the path I had cleared so meticulously. It would still be another two months until the snow would completely disappear, and I shoveled the path alone for the remainder of the season.

In the spring, the snow melted. The rivers and streams were no longer frozen, and the sound of birds returned to the trees. The air began to warm up, and the sun shone once again. Even so, the house felt empty. My mother said almost nothing and, on most days, could barely muster the energy to leave her room. The rooms hung there with an eerie quiet, the walls now silent where they once reverberated with the sound of my father's voice. Although his voice was not particularly distinctive, there was a certainty in his tone that was uncommon. It simply never wavered.

On the second Saturday of the month, I woke up early, went down to the kitchen and made sandwiches to take with me. I packed up the supplies and made sure I had plenty of water. I had checked the reels the night before and made sure that all of the equipment was intact, and that I had everything I needed for the day.

Almost overnight, it seemed I had aged. Inside, I was both hurt and hardened, the events of that morning embedded in my mind, playing over and over, unflinching. When I looked in the mirror, it seemed that a decade had been tacked on without consideration. And I now knew that the small space I had maintained for so long with normal teenage rebellion would now be filled with regret. Needless, unnecessary, eternal regret.

I no longer felt the need to prove myself to anyone, and so I did what men do, what men have always done.

I went out alone in a boat, with my thoughts pushed down deep, and cast my line into the quiet, dark waters with the sun at my back, the day ahead, and the fish swimming for their lives beneath the surface.

I DIDN'T KNOW WHAT TO SAY, SO I JUST SAID THANKS

People knew Lonnie because they saw him outside our high school each morning, smoking cigarettes across the street. He was the kid who waited until the very last minute to enter the building, and sometimes he waited longer than that, strolling into the corridors completely unaffected after the bell had rung.

There were other people who hung out with him, but it was his crew. They had clearly gathered there to be around him, not the other way around. Lonnie had a presence, an uncommon poise, that wasn't often seen in kids his age. He wouldn't have been classified as typically handsome, but there was something about him that suggested he knew more than the rest of us.

In middle school, his parents had returned home one night to find him passed out drunk. He had gotten into their liquor cabinet and had apparently sampled his father's Scotch collection. There was no sign of a party. He didn't invite people over. They say they found him in the most decadent chair in the living room, passed out with an emptied highball glass in his right hand. It was something out of *Mad Men*. Lonnie could even make getting busted seem cool.

This didn't keep his parents from sending him away to a rehabilitation center. He was only fourteen, after all, and finding him passed out drunk was more than enough cause for his parents' strong reaction. Lonnie's enrollment in the program was immediate. He just vanished into another world. Everything we heard about that night came from someone else, and this only seemed to add to his mystique. Lonnie became something of an urban legend. The longer he was away, the more it grew.

When he appeared at high school the next year, he was quieter, harder, and he had grown taller and skinnier during his time away. He had always carried himself beyond his years. Now he didn't just look older, he looked weathered, with facial hair and unmenacing eyes that seemed to narrow just a bit. He looked like someone we'd only seen in the movies, a man who emerges after a lengthy stint in prison with the type of untouchable bravado that can't be manufactured. It made us want to be around him and a little afraid of him at the same time.

The high school girls were different. The darkness that surrounded Lonnie only enhanced his appeal. It wasn't so much a bad boy appeal as a world-weary knowingness that seemed to captivate the girls, especially the older ones. If there was an element of Lonnie to be feared, teenage girls were so blinded by his quiet charisma they didn't see it. He was just the kind of guy their fathers would have told them to avoid at all costs, and this only made him more desirable. One minute he was passed out drunk with a glass of Scotch in his hand, and the next minute he was James Dean. Lonnie seemed to take life as it came. The slower he moved, the faster it seemed life was thrust upon him. It was a strange phenomenon.

Everything about him was just a little different. Even the way he took a drag on a cigarette was different from the rest of us. He didn't hold it like a joint, and his lungs accepted the smoke as if they were born to poison themselves without a hint of remorse. Even the way he put the cigarette out was done with style. He would toss it on the ground, disinterested, step on it with the ball of his right foot and twist it back and forth as if he was just about to square off in a gunfight. Then he would sidle across the street and through the front door of the school he seemed to have outgrown even though he was only in the ninth grade.

He approached his classes with body language that went out of its way to signal an air of passive detachment. He appeared neither engaged nor combative. He sat in class with an almost unmistakable joy about the absurdity of it all—kids torturing themselves as if their lives depended on it, and teachers constantly scolding them in search of order and control. Nothing about this atmosphere appealed to Lonnie and so he simply took a different approach, one that was wholly unsettling for both students and teachers alike.

We could not understand how Lonnie was able to sit there each day, legs stretched out in front of him, with a wry smile as he watched the world go by. While he emoted very little, we got the sense this was like theater to him, that we were all "players in the play" and that he could enjoy the rare privilege of serving as the audience. It wasn't just his easy calm but his role as an amused spectator that was most unnerving.

Teachers were frustrated by Lonnie's behavior. He didn't misbehave, so the option of punishment was nonexistent. If called upon, he was often clever. When he didn't know the answer, he informed the teachers of just that. What made him unique was that he did so without a hint of embarrassment. He wasn't remotely embarrassed he didn't know the answer and when teachers admonished him or implored him to do his work, he just smiled wide and easy and said, "OK." If the teacher was attractive, he might say, "Yes, ma'am," with a touch of enthusiasm—sufficient to get a laugh from the rest of the class but not enough to be sent to the office. It was just a game to him, and he played it well. To the students, he was a legend. To the teachers, he was a discomfort. They were probably unsure of whether to pass him along (undeservedly) to the next grade or risk another year of awkward moments.

By senior year, Lonnie and I had become friends. He went to all the parties, and Carla Tannyson was having one on Saturday night. I wasn't invited to many parties, but I knew Carla from math class, and she had told me I was welcome to come. I wasn't cool. In fact, I was the antithesis of cool. I figured I might gain some level of acceptance if I showed up at the party with beer.

I had cobbled together a fake ID from a guy in our grade named JT, who made them for a small fee. It wasn't perfect, and it just sat in my wallet taking up space. I couldn't imagine it would be enough to pass inspection at a convenience store, but I felt cooler having it inside my wallet. Lonnie said it looked good. There might have been a hint of truth in his comment, but I was hardly convinced. The last thing I wanted to do was get turned down. That would be more embarrassing than showing up at the party with nothing ... or not going at all.

"Come on," Lonnie said. "I'll go with you to the convenience store on Beaumont tomorrow night, and you can pick up your beers."

Beaumont Avenue was about fifteen minutes from the school. Thirty years ago, it was a pretty happening place, with a decent nightlife and some cool storefronts. My parents used to talk about it sometimes. But now it was pretty run-down—one of those forgotten areas of a city that doesn't go bad overnight but dies a slow, inevitable death.

When we got to the convenience store, Lonnie told me what to do. "Don't go in there getting beer and a bunch of other stuff," he said. "Nobody buys beer with bubble gum, Gatorade, and Starburst. You need to look like you've done this before. Beer and a pack of smokes. That's all."

Even as Lonnie talked me through the steps coolly, I was perspiring. My pulse quickened and I had my doubts I could pull this off. I just didn't possess Lonnie's requisite bravado, even with my ID. The older I got, the more it seemed life was about bravado and confidence. You could fool someone into thinking you knew what you were doing if you did it with certainty. That may have been even more important than competence, and I lacked the outward posture to ever look certain about anything. Still, Lonnie had inspired me. Perhaps inspired isn't the right word, but he gave me the temporary courage to go through with something I surely would have backed out of were he not there.

"Alright," I said and slammed the door while Lonnie watched from the car.

I walked into the store with an external calmness I hadn't felt before and heard the bells jingle on the glass door behind me. I studied the St. Pauli Girls in the cooler. I hadn't really considered which brand I was going to purchase, but I liked the girl with the yellow hair and pigtails on the label. There was no one else in the store, and I grabbed the six-pack and walked to the register.

The woman behind the register was about a decade older than me, but she looked like she had lived a lifetime more—at least in terms of experience. She wore jeans and a black tank top that revealed just enough to allow you to dream, if only for a second. She was lean with straight brown hair, chocolate eyes, and a tattoo of a small dagger on the inside of her left wrist. She didn't have a shred of makeup on. It was clear she didn't need it.

Once I came back to reality, I remembered what I was there for. I set the beers down on the counter, glanced over her shoulder and said, "Beers and a pack of smokes. Newports," just like Lonnie had told me.

It sounded good. Much better than I thought I could do, and I could feel something changing inside me, a feeling of belonging ... of validity, like I was absolutely meant to be there buying beer. I don't know why, but for the first time in my life I felt ... legitimate.

"Can I see some ID?" she asked.

I reached for my pocket and handed her my fake ID. She looked down at the photo and date and then back at me, then down at the ID again before sliding it back to me across the counter.

"That will be six fifty-nine," she said.

I was really feeling it now. I pulled out a ten-dollar bill and said, "Here you go." She handed me the change, and I walked out of the store irrevocably altered. I opened the car door, passed the beer and smokes across to Lonnie, and started the car without a word. I am not sure what made me do it, but I peeled out of that parking lot.

That weekend, I showed up at Carla's party with a six-pack of St. Pauli Girl tucked neatly under my arm. Lonnie threw his arm around my shoulder, giving me instant credibility.

"My boy," he said as I handed him a beer. He introduced me to a few people and then Carla saw us walking into the kitchen where people had congregated. It seemed like Carla was seeing me for the first time or, at the very least, seeing me differently.

I liked Carla. She was nice and pretty. The kind of girl who was previously unlikely to glance in my direction. But I was a guy who had just bought a six-pack of beer—with a fake ID no less. I was now someone who was no longer afraid to be there, to be face-to-face with her.

"What's up, Carla?" I said, tipping my chin upward. "Nice party."

She smiled and said hello, almost as if she was glad to see me.

I had even impressed myself. I wasn't sure what came next, so I offered her a beer. She reached for it and placed her hands around the cold can, as her fingers brushed against mine. She bobbed her head to follow her, and we walked outside and sat on a picnic table in her backyard. I saw Lonnie nodding in approval as we moved through the crowd and out the sliding doors.

From that night on, time moved at a different speed. Carla became my first girlfriend and we shared the summer months before heading off to different colleges. Lonnie was getting ready to join the Navy and went through basic training in Virginia before being shipped out. I never saw him again, but someone told me he had met a Romanian woman and was living somewhere on the coast of Spain. Carla found a new boyfriend in college, and I moved on as well.

A few years after college, I returned home and was working for a small business in town when I went to a concert on a Saturday night. It was at a tiny club, and I was standing with some friends when I saw her. She was older now, probably in her mid-thirties, but I was sure it was her. The tattoo on her wrist was unmistakable. She was still lean with straight brown hair, although it didn't quite have the sheen I remembered. I tried to avert her glance when she caught me looking at her. Surely, she didn't remember one night when a high school kid bought beer for the first time.

I just kept looking forward, but I could see her pay the bartender out of the corner of my eye. She held her drink in her left hand and began shuffling to the right, clearly moving in my direction. Finally, she stood in front of me and said, "Six-pack and smokes," laughing through her lipstick as she said it. I didn't know what to say, and she seemed to sense this.

"You know, Lonnie set the whole thing up. He told me about you, and he liked you a lot. He hardly liked anybody, but he liked you. He really liked you, and he asked me to do this one favor for him, even though I was risking my job. It was a lot to ask, but I think he knew I'd say yes. He had never asked me for anything.

I was more than a decade older than him, but I didn't care. He was wild, like a real cowboy, but also a gentleman, and I loved him."

I didn't know what to say, so I just said thanks.

LOCALS

It was the closest bar to my hotel, and I stepped out in the night, crossed the quiet street, and dropped in for a quick drink. The door was heavy, wooden, with a coat of arms painted on the front. It was almost medieval, and it appeared as if it had taken a beating over the years. Most importantly, it looked like the type of place that served beer, so I stopped in for a pint.

Inside, the bar was positioned on the left. The bar was made of stainless steel, polished well but with some scratches. A line of leather barstools with wooden legs sat below, and there were some empty tables off to the right. The bartender was leaning back easily and chatting with the man at the end of the bar. The man at the bar was wearing grey slacks and a white dress shirt now open at the collar. His shirtsleeves were slightly rolled up, and it was clear he had made himself more comfortable at the end of the day. He was clean-shaven with short, dark hair and an air of professionalism. The bartender was dressed more casually, in blue jeans and a plaid flannel shirt. He was young, in his late twenties, over six feet tall and very well built. He had a thick beard for his age, but it was maintained well, groomed and orderly. There was a touch of red in it, and he could very well have been Irish. There was nobody else inside the bar. I might have felt as if I was interrupting if I wasn't so damned thirsty.

"Pint of Guinness, please," I asked the bartender.

He moved for the glasses without breaking his concentration on the conversation with the man at the end of the bar. He even kept his eyes on him while he poured my beer out of the tap, only glancing down to be sure he didn't spill it. He then set the pint on the wooden bar and said, "Here you go, mister."

"Thanks," I said.

The bartender walked back toward the man who was seated at the end of the bar. It was clear they knew each other, or were at least familiar with one another, and that they seemed eager to continue their conversation.

"Heard Shelby opened a new joint," the man remarked to the bartender.

"Yeah, on the other side of town," said the bartender. "Close to the new master-planned communities they've built."

"I'm sure it will do well," said the man.

"It ought to," said the bartender. "Shelby's had this place for over fifty years without expanding."

"Not exactly a risk taker, you're saying?" said the man.

"You could say that," said the bartender.

"I know some people who've moved out that way," said the man. "Got a pretty good deal on their homes they told me."

"Yeah, land is cheaper out there," said the bartender. "My wife wouldn't mind moving there now that we have a family. Our little apartment seems to have gotten a lot smaller, and she would like a house."

"I get that," said the man. 'Every woman wants a house, especially once they have a baby. Most men don't need much more than a TV."

"To me, a bigger house just seems like more work … and more money," said the bartender. "But she doesn't see it that way."

"I bet she doesn't," said the man. "So why aren't you working at the new place?"

"Mr. Shelby wanted me here," said the bartender. "You know they've been trying to wrestle this place away from him for years?"

"So I've heard," said the man. "Is that really true?"

The bartender finished polishing one of the glasses with a rag and stroked his beard, as if he was thinking of just how much to reveal. It was clear that the man at the bar had been here before, but the bartender hesitated slightly before responding. He suddenly felt more protective of Shelby.

"Well, for years, it had been your run-of-the-mill chains. Household names, like Starbucks and McDonald's. They were all willing to overpay considerably to get their hands on this piece of real estate," said the bartender. "They made Mr. Shelby offers that would have set him up for life, but he never considered them."

"Why not?" asked the man. "Doesn't he like money?"

"Sure," said the bartender. "He likes money as much as the next guy. But this place is personal to him. It's his.

Has his family crest on the wall. Besides, he told me he wouldn't know what to do with himself if he cashed out."

The man at the bar had finished his beer, and he was spinning the glass around in his hands looking quizzically at the few remaining suds in the bottom.

"So, what happened?"

"Well," said the bartender, "eventually, the corporations stopped asking. They realized that, as long as he was the owner, nothing would get him to sell and they looked somewhere else. From time to time, there would be a new inquiry, but they dissipated after a while."

"So, what's going on now?" asked the man at the bar.

"This is a different kind of adversary," said the bartender. "Fancy developer. He's bought up the entire city block with the exception of this place. His backers are a different type of investor, which makes this more complicated."

"What are you saying?" said the man. "I am not sure I understand."

"Let's just say they aren't afraid to apply pressure," said the bartender before pausing. "A different kind of pressure. The kind that doesn't merely ask, but rather seeks to convince, often painfully."

"How does the old man feel about that?"

"The old man doesn't scare easily," said the bartender.

"And you?" said the man at the bar.

"I've been with Mr. Shelby a long time," said the bartender. "Started working for him as a kid loading boxes out back. Owe him everything I have. I'm in for the long haul."

"Regardless of the consequences?" asked the man at the bar.

"Yes," said the bartender. "Loyalty is a trait that can't ever afford to consider the consequences."

"I admire you," said the man at the bar. "Shelby is lucky to have you."

The bartender took a moment to pause. The man at the bar had slowly evolved the conversation like someone with an agenda, someone with a bit more skin in the game. With each question, the bartender could see he was establishing an opposing position. The bartender couldn't tell if this was simply a word of caution or if there was something that connected him more concretely.

"Would you like another beer?" asked the bartender, moving the conversation in a different direction.

"One more, yes," said the man. "Thank you."

"Fella, would you like another?" the bartender asked, peering in my direction to let me know he hadn't forgotten I was there.

"Yes, thanks very much," I said plainly.

The bartender poured our beers out of the silver tap.

"I've been told this developer has the construction companies in his pocket," said the man at the bar. "Unions and politicians too. There's no stopping him, I tell you."

"You seem to know an awful lot," said the bartender.

"Well, I know a lot of people," the man stammered. "I've been doing business in this town for a long time."

"What kind of business is that?" asked the bartender, now asking almost accusingly.

"Legal," said the man. "Public and private sector. I do lots of licensing."

"Like the licensing for urban development?" asked the bartender.

"All kinds of licensing, really."

I had been sitting for some time. I kept trying to look forward or stare into the bottom of my glass, but I heard every word. The warm rapport I witnessed when I entered had changed. The dialogue had slowly grown more tense, and I sensed the man at the bar was there to assess the situation and, if needed, deliver a message. The bartender seemed to perceive this too, but Shelby had him working here for a reason. That much was clear. He was more cunning than he appeared, and it was clear he was something of an immovable object. He cut to the chase.

"What do you want?" the bartender asked matter-of-factly.

"I don't want any trouble," said the man. "I am not a confrontational man."

"But you are the messenger?" the bartender suggested.

"In a sense, yes," said the man.

"Well, I am not sure what you think you'll accomplish," said the bartender. "I plan on working here for a long time to come."

The man at the bar looked disappointed, if slightly impressed. He finished his beer and set the glass down on the stainless-steel bar with care.

"Don't forget," he urged, "there is a fine line between loyalty and stubbornness."

"Not really," said the bartender. "You can't be loyal without being stubborn."

"Perhaps," said the man, as he put one arm inside his coat and then the other. "But courage doesn't prevent foolishness," he added while placing his stylish cap atop his head.

"Us Irish have never understood the difference," said the bartender.

"Some might see that as a genetic defect," said the man.

"Or a gift," countered the bartender.

"I just do the licensing," said the man. "Permits, stuff like that. Nothing more."

"Then what are you worried about?" asked the bartender.

There was nothing else to say. Men had been fighting over turf since the beginning of time, and this was no different. Wolves still came in sheep's clothing, and trust wasn't any easier to come by. The past and the future always slammed up against one another, and locals saw the concept of adaptation as the very definition of failure. Better to face death than prolong it. And death, in one manner or another, felt like it was coming. It hung over the bar like a scrim of sound with a pungent odor. The dye had been cast.

I watched as the man stood abruptly, tipped his cap to the bartender, and disappeared into the night. It was time for me to follow, so I paid my bill and said thanks. The bartender, still raw from the conclusion of the conversation with the man, nodded slightly upward at me almost like an afterthought. I walked out the door.

Outside, I felt the night air on my face. It had gotten colder since I had entered the bar. I zipped my jacket up to the top, so that it covered the bottom of my chin. I turned left and walked the block lined with cement mixers. One after the other. Grey and ominous in the quiet.

If you weren't careful, you could be swallowed up in a pool of cement and never seen again. It happened countless times, and this was always a possibility. In the morning, when the sun came up, these machines would sound a not-so-subtle warning and pour new foundations in an old town.

ORVILLE'S

When I applied for a job at the filling station, Orville looked at me with healthy skepticism. He had known me for a long time, and he knew I came from a well-off family and didn't need to pump gas. I had just finished college and showing up here asking for a job probably seemed like an odd choice. Orville wasn't so much suspicious as surprised.

"You don't need to work here," he said. "You know that."

It was true. I did know that, and I could have worked anywhere. Or just about anywhere. In small towns, people know everything about everyone, and people knew my dad had money. He ran a very successful insurance business, and people were aware of this. In addition, my father wasn't known for his modesty, and it wasn't unlike him to be seen driving new, expensive cars. As for Orville's, Dad and I had been going there for years, and he knew my father well enough to, at the very least, exchange pleasantries with him.

"I am not trying to work anywhere," I responded flatly. "I'm trying to work here."

Orville looked at me, still unsure, not quite certain whether to feel patronized or flattered. I think, in an effort to legitimize the job (which was unnecessary) he said, "It won't be easy."

"I know," I said respectfully, and I could see that Orville understood my interest was genuine.

"Alright," he said enthusiastically. "Your father know about this?"

My father didn't know about this. Not yet. I hadn't told him I was coming to speak with Orville.

"Not yet," I remarked. "I wanted to speak to you first."

Orville was something of an institution in our town. He was an African American man in his seventies, and he'd been working at the same filling station since he moved to town just over fifty years ago. He started out washing car windows, but he worked his way up and he'd owned the place for years now, when the previous owner was desperate for someone to take it off his hands.

Orville was one of the first African Americans to settle in town, and people didn't make it easy for him in those early days. This was right on the heels of the Civil Rights Movement, and for every person in town who was glad to have a Black family move in, there were probably three others who would have preferred the town remain as White as possible. Orville didn't care. Or, perhaps a better way of describing Orville is to say that he wasn't going to be deterred by an overwhelming sentiment that he may have been unwanted.

Orville carried that unwavering attitude with him each day he arrived at the filling station for work. It was determination by detachment. No matter how personal an insult or offhanded a comment might be, he never seemed to take it personally. It was a job, and he made sure he was excellent at it, that the prices were fair, the facility was clean, and the items were stocked—from snacks at the mini-mart to wiper blades. Orville set out to run an efficient business, and he put all his effort into doing so.

This isn't to say he didn't care about customer service, only that it wasn't based on personal taste. In fact, customer service was the heart of the business. Orville set a tone that was always kind and respectful yet professional. He greeted each customer with "Good day" followed by "ma'am" or "sir" as he had been taught by his own father. When he was out from behind the counter, he always made sure to hold the door and be courteous—even when he knew it might be followed by a racist remark under a customer's breath as they exited. He simply went back to his work, organizing the shelves, sweeping the floors, and manning the register. This impervious, utterly dignified demeanor endeared him to most, swayed others, and frustrated those insufferable racists who wished they could get to him. But Orville always maintained his composure, and he inspired me.

When I finished college, my parents asked me what I was going to do. I had been a good student and had obtained a degree in business management from the overpriced private university I was fortunate to attend. Many of my friends had gone to work in big cities for consulting firms or financial institutions. This was viewed as some measure of success, not merely for the students who had worked hard to obtain their degrees but for the parents who had worked hard to finance their educations. It wasn't necessarily an expectation as much as a strong hope. But this didn't seem like it was for me, and so I returned home after graduation to think about what I wanted to do next.

Once my father got past his initial disappointment, he came to me with a proposition. He had a job opportunity for me. It would be challenging. I would start at the bottom, but there was lots of potential for growth, and the starting salary was decent. I would be working for him, learning the family business, groomed until the day I was ready to take over once he retired.

In many ways, this was a great offer, an almost irresistible offer. My father knew this, and I am sure he never expected any hesitation on my part. He certainly didn't think I would turn it down, even though I knew I had to. It wasn't even a decision for me. This isn't to take anything away from my father or his business. I admired his accomplishments, and I knew that every opportunity I ever had was due to his hard work and the business he had built. Still, I knew what I had to do, and I did it as respectfully as one can ever do something that will potentially be taken as disrespectful and certainly ungrateful.

"Dad," I said. "I can't tell you how much I appreciate the job offer, but I have to turn it down. I am grateful, but I need to make it on my own."

"If you wanted to make it on your own, why didn't you take a job in the city?" he said with more than a touch of frustration, resentment even.

"It's hard to explain," I said. "I realize that most of my friends aren't here, and they aren't coming back. And I understand that you and Mom didn't spend all this money on my education just so I could come back here. But I am appreciative of everything you've done for me and for all of my opportunities. I was just ready to come home."

"Well, don't expect to lie around here, living rent-free, staring at your phone all day," said my dad.

I didn't say it at the time, but this was just the type of condescending remark that only reinforced the idea that I had to make it on my own. I had to get out from under that massive shadow, forceful, tough talk, and considerable legacy. Four years ago, I would have been inclined to respond defensively, but I had grown up a lot at college, and I just took the cheap shot on the chin. "Yes, of course, Dad. I wouldn't think of taking advantage of you and Mom. Can you give me a month to get a job and secure an apartment? Does that sound reasonable?

My dad looked at me skeptically. Was I trying to pull something over on him? Was I mocking him? I could tell he doubted my ability to obtain a job, and he looked at me like I was still an insecure kid and not a young man who could be taken seriously. But I wasn't laughing. I wasn't laughing at all, and I repeated my question. Does one month sound fair?

Now he wanted to respond. I could sense something snarky along the lines of "Did I think it would be that easy?" or "I had no idea what the real world was like" or something like that, but I cut my dad off when he opened his mouth to speak. "I am completely serious," I said, and there was nothing for my dad to do but agree even though it was easy to see he was wholly convinced that I would be sitting on the same couch in one month's time.

I waited a week to tell my parents about my job working for Orville. We sat down to dinner, just the three of us. Mom had made pork chops, which was Dad's favorite, along with a side of potatoes and a nice salad. We exchanged the normal pleasantries about our respective days, and we hadn't discussed the conversation from the week prior or the urgency surrounding my need to obtain a job. Mom could feel the tension, and she preferred to keep things light, particularly when she had gone to the trouble of making such a nice meal.

I knew there would never be a safer environment for me to share the news. Plus, I was excited. This was my first real job. I had obtained the opportunity completely on my own, and I was proud of it. I had always admired Orville. He always struck me as a man of uncompromising principles. Furthermore, he was classy and hardworking, and I was genuinely looking forward to the chance to learn from him.

After we passed the food around the table, I decided to break the silence and said, "I have something to share. I got a job, and I start next week."

I saw my dad send a look of skepticism in the direction of my mom. She received his message and turned her head back toward me. "Congratulations," she said. "That's very exciting."

I thanked my mom and told her I was excited about it. "I've got a couple of appointments to look at apartments this weekend," I added, making sure that my father also realized I would be honoring the commitment I made to find my own place despite his considerable doubt. He stayed silent and just continued eating his meal. It was always good, and my mom really put everything into this dish.

"Where are you working, honey?" asked my mom in a positive tone.

"I got a job working at Orville's," I said. "I interviewed with him last week."

My dad didn't say a word. I could see him momentarily stop eating when he heard Orville's name, but he quickly returned to his plate of food as if he was completely unsurprised by the news.

"Orville's?" repeated my mom, trying to keep the conversation going. "That's nice," she added politely.

"Yeah," I said. "I am looking forward to working there."

I had been waiting to see how long my dad could hold back, and I could see it wouldn't be much longer. The dinner had started off tense to begin with, and it had only become more awkward when I shared the news of my newfound employment. It was building inside him, and it was only a matter of time before he let it out. I was ready for it. There had been times in the past when I hadn't been ready. But I was ready now, and I just waited.

"So, we sent you to private school and college so you could work at a gas station?" he asked. "Is that what you are telling us? Really?"

There was incredible condescension in his tone, an air of superiority that was woven tightly into the fabric of his DNA, but I never thought it looked uglier than it did at that moment.

I was about to respond when my dad beat me to it. "And have you noticed that everyone who works at Orville's is Black?" he added really trying to pile on now.

"Not anymore," I said smugly before adding, "I thought you liked Orville."

"I do," said my dad.

"Then what's the problem?"

There are moments when conversations end simply because there is nowhere else to go or because you both know there is only one place to go. This conversation could have been categorized either way, and both of us refrained from saying another word for the entire meal. Mom tried to break the ice, but silence was as close as we were going to come to harmony on this occasion.

This meant that we ate in silence, the only sounds in the room belonging to cutlery making contact with our plates. But the contentious conversation wasn't for nothing. It had made an impact on my father, even if he would never admit it. But I think he saw me, perhaps for the first time, as formidable, able to speak for myself and willing to hold my ground—even in the face of his imposing persona. I showed up for work at Orville's the next morning, and a couple of weeks later I moved into my studio apartment.

On my first day of work, I arrived early, nearly an hour before the gas station opened. I figured I would be there before Orville, but I wanted to show him I was responsible, and I certainly didn't want to be late. As it turned out, Orville was already there. He was prepping the store, making sure everything was stocked, checking to see the shelves were lined in perfect order, and double-checking that the pumps were working and the registers, card readers, and payment options were all in good working order.

The entire place looked immaculate. The bathroom was spotless, and I could tell he had already cleaned it even though it was likely left in good order from the night before. All those years of stopping by, and I had always taken for granted that things were where they were supposed to be. I'd never really stopped to consider the work that went into it. From the first day, I learned that Orville was meticulous and purposeful. Everything was situated where it was for a reason. His place was the result of pride and hard work, and there wasn't a single sign of complacency. Anywhere.

"Why don't you make sure the buckets outside are filled with soap and water," Orville asked me. "People often clean their windows in the morning when they realize their cars are dirtier than they thought."

My shift hadn't started yet, but that didn't matter. I was there, and Orville assumed that, if I was there, I was there to work. "Got it," I said, and I stepped outside to prepare the buckets in the dark air, with the sun just beginning to rise in the distance.

From the beginning, Orville went out of his way to make it clear that we were no longer friends. We were colleagues, despite the fact that he had known me since I was a little kid. But I wasn't stopping in for a Gatorade after Little League. I was working, with him, alongside him, and for him. Orville knew it was important that we established a professional relationship. And it was empowering for me to be treated like a professional, an employee who needed to earn his keep. If my dad constantly made me feel like an unworthy kid, Orville made me feel like a man. I wanted to work hard for him, and I was proud to show up there each morning.

The job was harder than I thought. It came with its own complexities. It entailed far more than cleaning toilets or working the register. And, truth be told, it required quite an agile and creative business mind to manage ordering and purchasing, budgets, cash flow projections, and taxes. Beyond this, it required careful research of oil and gas markets, both foreign and domestic, and it became clear to me very quickly that Orville hadn't stayed in business for all these years by accident. He was as meticulous with numbers as he was with his shelves.

Even so, people were still at the core of the business. If you didn't have customers, the other aspects of the business would be rendered irrelevant. But it wasn't just customers that made the business successful. It was repeat customers. Our town was small, and it didn't take in much revenue from tourism or even people just passing through since it was far enough off the freeway to be an inconvenience. Getting people to return day after day, week after week, and year after year was what Orville needed to do in order to be successful over the long haul. This wasn't easy for anyone, let alone one of the first Black men in a predominantly White town. But Orville built his following on fair prices, the selection in the store, and the respect he demonstrated for all of his patrons.

I had been working there about a month when it started. Everything had been going well. I'd been working hard, showing up on time, and I was learning something new from Orville nearly every day. He was very generous with trying to teach me about the business. More importantly, he was just an easy person to admire. Beyond the professional manner in which he ran his business, he was just such an honorable and decent guy. He was careful not to blur the lines between employment and friendship, but it was clear that our relationship was growing the more he realized he could really count on me.

It was an unusually hot day just before the start of summer when the man walked into the store. Orville was behind the register and I was stocking the shelves when the man walked by me and said, "Boy, you should be ashamed of yourself, working for a *nigger*. You're a disgrace to your family."

After getting over the initial shock, I was about to respond in defense of Orville. However, before doing so, I looked over at Orville and saw him shake his head "no" despite my anger.

I took a deep breath and asked the man, "Sir, can I help you with anything?"

"Didn't you hear me, son?" he repeated. "You see any other White boys working here? What the fuck are you doing?"

By now, I had transitioned from anger into the mode of professional detachment Orville had taught me so well.

"If you don't need anything, sir, I am going to return to stocking the shelves," I said flatly. "Thanks for coming in."

Orville had been right. The man looked at me in utter disbelief, shook his own head, and headed to the register to pay Orville and walk out without saying a word. He had been rendered speechless by my impervious nature, and Orville repeated what he had shared before.

"In life, you can never allow people to think they are getting the best of you, that they have found your vulnerabilities. If you do, they'll exploit them and never let up," repeated Orville. "The key, I think, is to appear untouchable. A foolish man might mistake this feigned indifference for weakness, but it's just the opposite. Nothing makes a stronger statement than being wholly unaffected by a verbal attack."

He was right. Of course, he was right. But it was impossibly hard to bite my tongue. Still, it was a test.

Orville knew these attacks were coming. He knew when he decided to hire me. It's why he said the job wouldn't be easy. He had been through far worse, but he knew people in town wouldn't make it easy on me. After all, this was still the South, and progress was slower here.

What Orville hadn't considered was that my working for him might have a negative effect on his business. However, after a few months, it was clear that fewer people were coming to Orville's. His numbers were down, and the only change had been my hiring.

The reasons for this boycott of sorts were likely more complex than I might have imagined. Unfaithful husbands, who might have stopped at Orville's to pick up a bottle of White Zinfandel for their girlfriends, now had to consider that I worked there, that I might know their families, and that they couldn't go to Orville's as anonymously as they once could. They knew their secrets were safe with Orville, but I was seen as different. There were others who might have been put off by the integration of races, by a kid from one of the wealthiest, White families in town working for a Black man, like it was setting the White race back in some demented way. It was complicated, but there was no question that business had decreased since Orville had hired me.

As long as I continued to do my job well and work hard, I had the feeling that Orville would never say anything to me. But I felt bad. I felt guilty, and the last thing I ever wanted to do was hurt Orville's business by my presence. Even if he had faced more than his share of racism, his business had been solid for decades. The idea that I might be hurting it was more than I could handle, and I went to speak with him about it.

The solution seemed obvious to me, and I offered to resign from my position, so that Orville's could go back to the way it was, so that the bottom line could straighten itself out. And I thanked him genuinely for the opportunity he had given me.

Orville listened carefully and then spoke. "If you want to quit, I can't stop you, but I won't fire you or accept your resignation. You have done a good job, and I am pleased with the way you have worked. You've been a good employee."

Much as I appreciated Orville's kind words, his approach made no sense to me. He had worked for decades to build his business, and the last thing I wanted to do was destroy it in a matter of months. Moreover, he had taught me quite a bit about the economics of running a small business in the time I had been there, and this just seemed like a business decision to me, and one with a relatively obvious solution.

"Orville," I said. "You told me never to let my emotions run my business decisions."

"That's true," said Orville. "I did make it clear that emotional decisions are not often rational ones. But this decision isn't guided by emotion or sentimentality."

"If it's not emotion, then why would you make a choice you know isn't good for the business."

Orville waited longer than usual before responding. I had the feeling he knew what he wanted to convey, but he seemed to feel it was important to convey this in just the right manner. He massaged the sides of his mouth with his right hand, took a deep breath, and then answered in a calm, measured tone.

"While emotion should never guide you, there is one thing, from time to time, which must compete with economic decisions: *principle*. Yes, there are times when principle earns the right to compete with economics. And this is one of those times."

He stopped there and paused.

"Are principles worth losing your business over?" I asked.

"What kind of boss would I be if I fired my best employee because of the color of his skin? Because that would be the reason. If we have fewer Black customers, it's because you are a White kid. If we have fewer White customers, it's because you are a White kid." he reiterated.

"Yes," I said. "But you've swallowed your tongue before. You've held your principles in check to deal with racist customers over the years."

"That's different," Orville noted. "My principles guided me at those times too. I relied on them to run my business, treat people equally, and be undeterred by their beliefs. It was my principles that guided me to focus on the job itself. I wasn't swallowing my principles so much as clinging to them. This is no different."

"Are your principles worth going down with the ship?" I asked.

"Well, this ship has been sailing a long time," said Orville. "If it has made it this far on principle, I am going to have faith, even if it's blind faith, that it will make it on principle again. If not, at least I can be proud of how I have run the business."

To his credit, Orville stood on his principles and he stood his ground. With time, things began to change, and business started to come around. No matter how much it might have bothered people that I was working for Orville, they made economic decisions too. Orville had the fairest prices in town, and our store had the widest variety of goods. Most people simply couldn't afford to pay more forever, and they probably just hoped Orville would fire me or I'd quit. But Orville had outlasted them, the way he always had, and slowly his customers returned.

Even though I had my own place now, I still went over to Mom and Dad's for dinner once a week. There was little doubt that they received an earful from some of their friends, and for this I was sorry. I had never meant to make their lives more difficult, and I hadn't foreseen the ripple effect my working for Orville might have throughout our town. Still, Mom and Dad tried not to make me feel bad, and they asked me about the job, what I had learned, and how I liked working for Orville. I shared, with enthusiasm, that the job had taught me more than I could have hoped, and that Orville was a fair and very decent man to work for.

"I am glad you are enjoying the job," said my mom. And my dad chimed in about Orville, "You already knew he was a good man."

"Thanks, Mom," I said. "And yes, Dad, that's true. But it's different when you work for someone. You see different sides of a person and the relationship changes, but my admiration for Orville has only grown."

One noticeable absence since I began working for Orville was that my father hadn't stopped in at the station for gas. My mom rarely went to that area of town, but Dad's business took him everywhere, and he had been a pretty regular customer before I started working there. Still, he had come around regarding the job for the most part, and I wanted to be respectful when I asked him about why he hadn't come around.

"Dad?" I asked with more sensitivity than I had shown when I was seeking my independence. "You haven't come by Orville's since I have been working there."

My dad looked at me without a shred of anger. If anything, his eyes looked more worn and tired than I remembered. There was some pain in them, and I could tell the answer summoned varied emotions.

"Well," he remarked, almost apologetically. "It's more complicated than you might imagine. People around these parts haven't made it easy on your mother and me, and I figured I didn't want to cause you or Orville any problems either."

His response was reasonable and genuine. It could have seemed like a cop-out, but I knew my dad, and I knew when he was being honest. And I could tell he didn't want to cause any trouble, for Orville in particular.

"I can appreciate that, Dad," I said. "You looking out for everyone else. But I know Orville would enjoy seeing you. He asks me how you are doing, and I'd look forward to showing you where I work."

He nodded and said he'd try and stop by before too long.

Business continued to pick up. The rise was slow but steady, and Orville's numbers were returning to the levels they had been at before he made the decision to hire me. It was now the middle of summer, and the temperatures were warm, very warm. This always helped the store, and kids would stop in for cold drinks on summer break once school let out.

Orville gave me a shirt with short sleeves that was modified for summer. One of the biggest challenges of the job for me was making sure that my uniform was ready each morning. I had never had a uniform for school, and I learned quickly that it took a degree of work to make sure my clothes were clean and wrinkle-free each day.

Orville seemed to have no such problems. His hair was neat. He was always clean-shaven. And his clothes were immaculate, clean, and pressed without a single crease. Even the collars lay exactly the way they were supposed to. Orville did it all himself these days. He had been a widow for seven years, and his children had never returned after going to college. He had a son who lived in Charlotte, another who lived in Atlanta, and he had lived alone since his wife passed away.

Beyond my admiration for his shirts, Orville and I were becoming friends. Although work was busy at times, there were also quiet moments when Orville wasn't focused on teaching me the business. In those moments, we talked like colleagues, like two men who were becoming more comfortable with the idea of getting to know one another better, and with real affection despite our age difference. Orville was always professional, but I think I had proved my worth enough to establish a working relationship that now bled, healthily, into the personal as well.

"Do you miss your sons?" I asked one day.

"Of course," said Orville. "But they are moving forward and living their lives. That's a good thing."

"They never wanted to come back here?" I asked. "Take over the family business?"

"No," responded Orville. "That was never going to be the case. They saw too much, heard too much as children to want to take this on or live in this small town. They were ready to seek something more."

"How has that worked out for them?" I inquired.

"It's been good," responded Orville. "I think it's been what they hoped for, the city, with more people who look like they do. In a sense, it's almost made them forget about this place, but that's OK. The world goes on."

"And you?" I asked. "Do they come home to see you?"

"Not all that much," said Orville. "And less since their mom died. They each offered me the chance to retire and move in with their families, but this is my home."

"Are you still happy here?" I asked. "Without any family in town."

"I've always been happy here," Orville responded convincingly. "And I know the game. Kids are supposed to move away from their parents. They are supposed to become independent, and sometimes the best thing they can do, in order for that to happen, is forget where they came from."

"Why?"

"So, they can go on," said Orville. "Otherwise, they often can't, and they drown in guilt and sorrow and pain and loss that are always attached to the place you grow up. It's OK. I made peace with this long ago."

I knew I was probably traveling into territory where I should not venture, but the day was slow, impossibly slow, and I could tell Orville felt like talking. "Ever think of remarrying?" I asked.

"Nope," said Orville. "That's not for me. There have been interested women, but I was lucky enough to find the right woman once, and that's more than enough until we meet again."

"Doesn't it get … lonely?"

"It does, but that's how life works sometimes. And just because I might get lonely doesn't mean I should look for companionship now that my wife has passed on," he said confidently.

"But don't you have to change when life lowers the boom and alters your reality?" I asked.

"No," said Orville. "I don't think you do. In fact, I am certain that you don't need to change, not if you've lived a good life. Just because the circumstances change doesn't mean you should do anything different. I think that's a common myth. Everyone thinks you have to adapt, but you don't. *You just have to keep going.* That's what you really have to do. Keep going. So, you lose some things. So, you lose some people. So what. Why should that change your approach? It might make your life less fulfilling, less enjoyable, but it doesn't require or demand change."

His words were strong and impassioned. He was composed, but he spoke with conviction and a hint of raw emotion he rarely displayed. He wasn't just principled. He was courageous in his own way.

"Well," I said. "My dad's always adjusting to changes. He likes that mantra that says you either adapt or die."

"With all due respect to your father," said Orville, "that's just impatience."

"Well, patience is certainly not his forte," I agreed.

"Well, patience isn't easy, and it's not for everyone," added Orville. "But if you know who you are, and you know why you do the things you do, what is the motivation to change? Right things are still right even when things don't go as planned."

The day was getting on, and it was near closing time. Orville and I had spent much of the afternoon talking, in between sparse customers. The sun had gone down, and the air was now nice and cool. I went outside to lock up the bathrooms, while Orville began to tidy the store before closing out the register.

We could see lights approaching in the distance. Orville waited to close out the books for the day, since it looked like we would have one last customer. As the car inched closer, Orville turned to me and said, "I am going to let you close up tonight." He then stepped out of the door, bent slightly at the waist, tipped his cap to the driver of the car that pulled in, and was off.

As Orville disappeared into the dark night, I watched the silhouette of my father, illuminated by the overhead light of the gas station, step from the car and enter the store.

SOUTHERN HOSPITALITY

Dusty Wingate used to fix the slot machines at the casino, back when he lived in Loughlin, Nevada. He was good at it too, and this made him a pretty valuable commodity with a useful skill set in a place where casinos were plentiful.

But all good things come to an end, and this was no different. Dusty got greedy, decided to take a little extra something for himself. A little off the top. It wasn't all that much, just a taste, a chance to get his hands on what he thought he was worth, what he thought he was owed. And he probably was. Still, it was more than he was entitled to, and you can't cross that line (even by the smallest margin) if you are going to survive in the casino business.

America is a big country, but there are only so many places you can go when you leave Nevada on bad terms, and on bad terms with the wrong people. They will find you in California, whether you are tucked up in a hole in LA or driving with the top down along the Monterey Peninsula. Your best chance is to head to the Southeast. Make it to the other side of the Mississippi and disappear below the Mason-Dixon line.

White men have done this for decades, seeking refuge in the South where Sherman once marched to the sea and the emancipation proclamation was met with resistance. These men have ranged from Nazi guards from World War II to disillusioned ironworkers from the Midwest. All they needed to do was follow a couple of simple, straightforward rules. Keep to yourself. Keep quiet. In essence, have some respect and know your place. Do these things and Southerners will eventually embrace you as one of their own.

Unlike other Americans, Southerners aren't interested in your history. They're interested in theirs. And they will pretty much give you a clean slate. Just show up. Get to work. And make yourself useful. Dusty was nothing if not useful. His talents weren't confined to a casino. He was the kind of guy who could do just about anything with his hands. From rebuilding carburetors to fixing toilets, Dusty had it covered. He could put in your drywall or your air conditioning, refinish your floors or upholster your couch.

He wasn't nearly as good at marriage. He'd been married four times in all, and each union had ended remarkably similarly, when his wives became fed up with him and his behavior for good reason. It was surprising that he could convince another woman to take a chance on him after so many failed attempts, but Dusty was charming and handsome in a way that was manly if not pretty. The strong and silent type. Few words but all of them chosen wisely. Truth was each of his wives thought they could change him. Otherwise they wouldn't have taken the plunge. Dusty knew this wasn't possible but, so long as they believed it was, he wasn't going to try and convince them otherwise. After all, he enjoyed the company of women, even if they would learn in time that he wasn't worth it. For a man from Nevada, Dusty was a bad bet.

The women in the South were different, and Dusty could sense this from the moment he arrived. The first night he pulled into town, it was late. He was hungry. He was very hungry, and he headed to the Waffle House. He only knew it by reputation, but he knew enough to know that it was open all night long. He slid into the booth easily, almost like a young kid would do, and looked over the menu with enthusiasm. He had to admit it was pretty impressive and more comprehensive than he had imagined. It was hardly confined to just waffles, and Dusty liked the idea that he could get steak and eggs alongside his waffles anytime day or night.

The waitress came over to his table smiling. Even at two in the morning, she was smiling, and she pulled a pencil out from behind her ear just the way they did in the old movies he watched. She was chewing gum, with her blonde hair pulled up. It was too perfect. She was too perfect and, if you didn't know it, you would have thought she was in costume. But she was real. She was all too real, and Dusty was captivated from the moment he saw her.

"Can I start you off with something?" she asked with a sweet voice, big brown eyes, and a sexy, Southern drawl that could melt a stick of butter.

"Cup of coffee," said Dusty. "Black."

"Yessir," she responded with a smile. "Sit tight, sugar. I'll be right back."

Dusty looked around the restaurant. He couldn't believe it was so full at this hour. The lights inside were bright and glowing, as if it could have been the middle of the day. However, a look at the windows, which were black from the night sky outside, told a different story. But here, under the lights, with the smell of grease and butter and bacon wafting off the grill, even the most intoxicated patron or exhausted traveler could be brought to life, awakened, in the company of warm strangers and the comfort of warm food.

The Waffle House was quite a scene in the early morning hours. It had it all, really. The plumber who had just made a house call. The young guys who had just come from the bar, drunk, unlucky with women, and hungry from the night. An old couple who likely had woken up in the middle of the night, as old people are prone to do. Girlfriends who'd ended up there after a night out on the town. The priest, with his white collar slightly loosened. A young family with a baby girl in a stroller, asleep next to the table, perhaps finally closing her eyes amidst the din of voices and the clanking of plates.

If Dusty was looking to swindle someone or pick a pocket, this lot would have been there for the taking. They weren't so much vulnerable as comfortable, overwhelmingly comfortable, and they would have been wholly unsuspecting that someone conniving could arrive in a place of so much, well … goodness.

It was just a passing thought, and Dusty wouldn't have thought of taking advantage here. There was something different about these people, all of them. They weren't trying to get a leg up, get ahead, or step on anyone's throat to climb a ladder. They were just there, in content trances, sitting over plates of food like an offering from the gods. They were fully present, satisfied, and they acted as if there was no place on earth they would rather be—right there, at those laminate tables, eating, at that moment.

Dusty found a job in no time, working at LJ's Filling Station over on High Street. He looked like every other grease monkey when he walked in, and they had him pumping gas that afternoon. No long application or interview. No background check. All that was important was that Dusty could do the job, and it only took him a few minutes to prove he was more than capable. By week's end, he had a blue shirt with an STP patch on the pocket, LJ's on the back, and Dusty scrawled in white script on the front left breast. Most of all, Dusty liked that he could still wear his cap with the mesh in the back. It wasn't standard issued, but it might as well have been.

Dusty started out pumping gas. They still had stations in the South with full serve, and LJ's was one of them. Customers counted on this, and he was more than happy to check their oil and wash their windshields. After all, he was getting paid. Nobody was chasing him down. He might not have been using his skill set to the fullest, but he was making ends meet. He got a little apartment in town and bought a small TV.

LJ was a pretty entrepreneurial guy. He was now in his late sixties, with gray hair that was parted to the side below his ball cap. He still wore a ball cap, but he always parted his hair beneath it. He was the boss, but he wore the same shirt as everyone else, except his said LJ on the front and the back. But he wanted to appear no better or worse than anyone else, and he walked the walk. LJ wasn't afraid to get his hands dirty either, and he enjoyed crawling under a chassis whenever he got the chance.

When LJ bought the place, it was just a gas station. But he added a service department, where people could get everything from an oil change to a new transmission. People liked to come to LJ's. He was an honest guy. His mechanics were good. And they turned wrenches all day long.

One morning, a few months after he started, Dusty came to work when the service department was a man short with a considerable backup of jobs. Usually, LJ would assist when someone was out, but his back was bothering him.

"Dusty," said LJ. "Think you could help the boys out today?"

"Yessir," said Dusty. "Happy to."

The guys shared some skeptical glances. They were a tight crew, but they were also happy to have the help. Dusty nodded in his unassuming manner and just asked what he could do to help.

"Can you handle a wheel alignment and a couple of oil changes?" said Danny, hoping Dusty had enough prior experience to take these on. "That would be a big help today."

"Sure," said Dusty. "I got it."

The boys nodded, and everybody went to work, including Dusty. Other than a couple of questions about the locations of parts and so forth, Dusty was self-sufficient, and the guys could all focus on their respective work. The day went pretty smoothly. They got everything done on time, and LJ thanked Dusty for pitching in before heading home.

"Anytime," said Dusty. He wasn't talkative, but he always seemed to say more than most in a few words.

As LJ pulled out of the parking lot in his old Cadillac, Dusty and the guys gave a quick wave. That Caddy was a good-lookin' horse, and it always got their attention.

"Dusty," called Danny. "Me and the fellas are gonna grab a couple beers before heading home. Wanna join us?"

Dusty thought about it for a minute. They'd never asked him before, and he pretty much kept to himself anyway. He liked it that way. And it just seemed simpler without people knowing much about his past. But he didn't want to be rude either, and this felt like an invitation he needed to accept.

"Sure," said Dusty.

Dusty liked the word "sure" a lot. In fact, "sure" might have been his favorite word, because it really embodied him. When you said "sure," it told people you were willing without needing to be convinced, that you were happy to do so without being overeager, and you didn't care more about anything than you should. That seemed to fit Dusty to a T, and he responded with "sure" just about every chance he got.

The bar was just down the street. Dusty had passed it dozens of times, but he had never stopped there. He was always ready to get home at the end of a long day, stay under the radar, and get on with it. In fact, the only place he went regularly outside of work was the Waffle House. That had become his joint, in part because of the food, in part because nobody seemed to notice him even in a crowded room, and in part because she worked there. He still would have gone if she hadn't worked there, but knowing she'd be there made the Waffle House the highlight of his day.

From the outside, the bar was rustic, wooden, and in need of a paint job. The inside showed its years as well, but it was surprisingly clean. Dusty noticed this right away, and it was clear the owner took real pride in the presentation. The barkeeps wiped down the bar repeatedly. The floor was swept well, and the restrooms had fresh towels. These were little things, but they made a difference.

Most of all, the bar was stocked. This wasn't a place for dancing. It was a place for drinking, and their catalog reflected this. Multiple brands of vodkas and gin and more brands of whiskey than you could count. The wine collection was minimal, but they had plenty of beers, mostly American, on tap. Most of the patrons were men, which wasn't surprising, since there wasn't a feminine touch anywhere to be found. Still, there was a table of women in the corner and a couple more sitting at the bar. The guys from LJ's settled into a booth, and Danny ordered the first round.

"Thanks for helping out today, Dusty," said Danny. "We appreciate it."

"Sure," said Dusty.

"You don't talk much, do you, Dusty?" added Henry, the youngest of the group.

"Not much," responded Dusty. "Unless I have to."

"Well, you don't have to here," said Elton, "so long as you buy a round when it's your turn."

"Fair enough," said Dusty.

"So … where you from, Dusty?" said Elton, and everyone laughed as he kept the questions coming.

"Here and there," said Dusty without a hint of a smile.

"Got yourself a lady?" inquired Steve, who was pretty quiet and seemed most like Dusty.

"Nah," shrugged Dusty.

"But you're a good lookin' fella," added Steve.

"That's what they tell me," snapped Dusty.

Smirks surrounded the table. Dusty was a pro, and he'd been around. He was quick and much sharper than the guys might have imagined when they first sat down after work. Dusty wasn't being unfriendly, and he was more than happy to field as many questions as they wanted to pose to him. But he wasn't going to reveal much, certainly not more than he chose to reveal.

"What brought you to South Carolina?"

"The accents," said Dusty.

"Why did you apply for a job at LJ's?"

"Thought it stood for 'Looking for a job,'" joked Dusty.

"Where do you like to eat?"

"The Waffle House."

"Why?"

"I like waffles."

Dusty could do this all day, now laughing, good-natured and loosening up, but no closer to sharing anything of real value. The guys had to either be pissed off, impressed, or accept it. And Dusty was a hard guy to be pissed off at to be honest—at least at first glance. He was always up to lend a hand, throw back a shot, or buy a round. And he knew a heck of a lot more about cars than he let on. He was a man's man if nothing else.

Dusty brought the waitress over without even raising his hand. Just a glance, and a slight tilt of his head and lift of his eyebrows was all it took to send her past a sea of outstretched arms and over to their table.

"Dadgum!" said Elton.

"Impressive," chimed Danny.

The waitress was young and cute, far too young for Dusty. Too young to even be influenced by his gaze. But there she was standing next to him at their table in tight jeans and a small, sleeveless top.

"Hey, fellas," she said. "What can I get y'all?"

She leaned down and whispered something into Dusty's ear to the absolute dismay of the others.

Dusty smiled, looked at her, and said, "Sure."

"What did she ask you?" said Henry.

"She wanted to know if you were old enough to be in here with us," smiled Dusty. The waitress played coy while the others laughed.

"Funny," deadpanned Steve.

"Another round of beers," said Dusty. "And four shots of Jack Daniels as well."

"Right on," said the waitress before she jumped in. "Do I know you from somewhere?"

"Don't think so."

"Really?" she asked again. "You look familiar."

"I'm not from around here, miss."

"I know I have seen you before," she said.

"Must have one of those faces," said Dusty.

The waitress just shrugged, unconvinced, and walked toward the bar to get their drinks ordered. The men took a long look at her as she walked away. They weren't so much acting perverted as intoxicated by her beauty. In some parts of the country, it might have been considered sexist to admire another person's physical beauty. But not in South Carolina. No, in the South it was still considered flattering to have your beauty admired. It was seen as an innocent compliment, and the waitress was obviously used to it. After all, she was beautiful, naturally beautiful, without a heavy dose of makeup or alterations. She was beautiful, and people must have noticed wherever she went. The men from LJ's were no different.

"So, what did she really say to you, Dusty?" asked Danny.

"I told you," said Dusty. "Checking IDs. Figured I was the oldest."

"That's bull," said Henry. "She's served me before. Come on, man."

"If you have to know," said Dusty. "She wanted to know what I was doing with you Neanderthals."

"You're a real comedian, Dusty," said Elton.

"So they tell me."

When the waitress returned from the bar with their drinks, she happened to catch a glimpse of Dusty with his head tilted slightly down, hat pulled over his eyes. That's when it came to her. It just popped into her head. Of course, it was him. How could she not have realized at first?

"The Waffle House!" she blurted out. "You go to the Waffle House every night!"

"Sure," said Dusty.

"Told you I knew ya," she said, feeling very pleased with herself.

"But how would you know that?" asked Dusty, not off guard, but curious at the very least how she knew this about him.

"Some of the girls from the bar go there after we close," she said. "You always sit alone at the counter, with your hat pulled down."

"Sure do. I like waffles," said Dusty, still unaware of how she knew how often he frequented the place.

Realizing the gap in her story, the waitress added, "Our friend Sandy works there, and she told us about you. She calls you 'The Gentleman.'"

"She must not know him very well," said Henry.

But Dusty paid no attention. He just kept his eyes steady, fixed on the waitress. He looked straight at her in a way that made her feel, she wasn't sure what, but something sincere. Then he smiled and just tipped his cap at her.

"Ma'am," he said humbly. "I try to mind my manners."

"I knew it," said the waitress. "I just knew it. I never forget a face."

She headed back to the bar to manage the other orders that were building up while she chatted with Dusty. The boys threw back their shots of Jack Daniels and Danny said, "To Dusty! Thanks … and welcome to LJ's."

Dusty nodded and said quietly, "Appreciate it."

They drank their beers. The bar was pretty crowded, and they sat back in their seats. It had been a long day, a very long day. Dusty wasn't looking for friends, not really, but the guys were nice enough and he couldn't complain. But he was ready to go. So, he finished his beer, threw down some cash, and told the fellas he was heading out. Dusty thanked them and stood up when Elton said, "Hey, Dusty, why do you go to the Waffle House in the middle of the night."

"Can't sleep," said Dusty.

"Where are you going now?" said Danny.

"To sleep," countered Dusty, pretty satisfied with himself. "Later, fellas," he said and walked toward the door. He caught the waitress's eye, and she cut him off at the door and whispered something in his ear. Then he was gone.

Dusty woke up about half past two in the morning. He had slept longer than usual. Probably that shot of Jack, he thought. Either way, he was awake. He was awake now, and he knew he wouldn't be able to go back to sleep. He used to sleep better, but now he woke up nearly every night. He wasn't sure if this was just because he was getting older or because he knew people were looking for him. Much as they were unlikely to find him here, he always held that thought in the back of his mind that they could. Add to that a few ex-wives and you don't sleep the way you once did.

Still, when he thought about Nevada, he didn't have any regrets. He wasn't a thief by nature. It wasn't in his blood. But he had a real problem with things that appeared unjust. Even if something was legal, it bothered him if it was unjust. In Loughlin, Nevada, he felt like he was on the wrong side of justice, and so he wasn't trying to pull a fast one so much as even up the score a bit. This approach did him no favors with ex-wives or bosses, but Dusty had his own code of ethics that he lived by, come what may. He had made peace with his internal constitution long ago, and he was willing to accept whatever consequences accompanied it.

When he got his head together, he swung his legs off the side of the bed and reached down for his boots. He had fallen asleep in his jeans, and so he just had to pull his boots on, grab his jacket that hung over the back of a kitchen chair, and pick up the car keys on the table. The Waffle House was just a couple of miles away, and he was starving. He often woke up starving, but it worked out since he usually had a pretty good appetite when he sat down to eat at the Waffle House. Even if he wasn't all that hungry, it never took more than the smell of grease and syrup and bacon on the griddle to awaken his senses.

It was after three o'clock when Dusty arrived, and there weren't too many people inside. He sat down and no longer needed to look at the menu. Sandy came over as soon as she saw him there.

"Hey, sugar. You alright?" she asked, since Dusty seemed to be staring blankly forward.

"Sure," he said.

"Well then, what can I get you? The usual."

"Yes, please," he said, stumbling over his words a bit. "Ma'am," he said and tipped his cap.

She smiled warmly. "It will only be a few minutes."

Dusty sipped his coffee and wiped the sleep from his eyes when he spotted a group of young women at a booth in the corner. The waitress from the bar was there, and he just shook his head. He had liked it better when he could be completely anonymous.

The waitress walked over to him at the counter. "Figured we'd see you here."

"What are the chances?" said Dusty sarcastically.

"So, why do you always sit at the counter?"

"Why not?" snapped Dusty.

"Because a booth's more comfortable," said the waitress.

"I like the view better from here," said Dusty. "You know. Sit up high. Watch the food be cooked."

"And talk to Sandy."

"You said it. But, yeah, sure."

"I am just messing with you," said the waitress. "Sandy told us she likes when you sit here. That way she can talk to you when she goes back and forth and when the crowd dies down."

"Is that right?"

"Yes, sir. Told us last week. Said she feels like she isn't so alone when you are here, like she's got a friend."

Dusty wasn't sure how he should respond. And that was unusual. It was unusual for him to be unsure and even more unusual for him not to know exactly how to respond. This time, the waitress had caught him off guard. Sandy made him feel like he had a friend too. She was the first person he met when he got into town, and he was glad it was her he met first. She wasn't just friendly in the way waitresses are who work hard for customers in hopes of a good tip. It was her nature. He had been around, and he knew the difference. She wasn't nearly as pretty as the waitress from the bar, but her nature was pure and sweet and kind, right down to her core. He could sense it the first time they spoke, and she put just a little more into everything—topping off a cup of coffee or just taking the time to ask a customer how they were doing, not just what they wanted. This was rare, and he liked Sandy. He liked her a lot.

"Talking to Sandy," said Dusty, "is the best part of my day."

"Well, there you have it," said the waitress.

"Wanna come over and meet my friends?" asked the waitress.

"Not especially," said Dusty.

"I know," said the waitress. "Just wanted to see what you'd say."

"You have fun with your friends," said Dusty.

The waitress whispered in his ear again before walking to her table. "She could use a good man," she said. "You be sure to treat her right."

"Yes, ma'am," Dusty drawled.

"What was that about?" asked Sandy as she topped off his coffee.

"Girl talk," deadpanned Dusty.

"I see."

Dusty's food was up, and Sandy turned and grabbed the plates, pivoted, and set them down in front of Dusty.

"Be right back, sugar," she said as she moved to the register.

Her friends had finished eating and were ready to leave. The waitress stood at the register with the check, while her friends cast their eyes upon Dusty, alone at the counter. Sandy closed them out and gave them their change. Dusty turned just in time to see the waitress wink and say, "See ya, Sandy," before turning to walk out the door with her friends.

There was no one left inside the Waffle House now. It was nearly four, and the cook headed outside to have a smoke. Outside, the black air surrounded the building, panes of glass aglow on a dark road with the world asleep. Sandy sat down on the barstool next to Dusty, took a deep breath, and buried her face into her arms that were folded across the countertop.

"I'm so tired," she said. "I'm just so tired."

"That's understandable," said Dusty. "You work all night."

Sandy took a glance upward and then over at Dusty before burying her head back in her arms. She kept her head down, resting against her arms, and he could hear her soft breathing against the countertop before she began to speak.

"We're becoming friends, Dusty, right?" she asked.

"We are friends," said Dusty. "Here in the South, you are my best friend."

"And I can talk to you?" she inquired further. "Like, really talk to you?"

"We talk every night," answered Dusty.

"I know we talk every night, sugar," she responded. "And bless your heart for listening. But this is different. I have a question to ask you."

"Sure," said Dusty casually.

"Promise you won't get mad?" she asked.

"Well, I don't get mad often," said Dusty. "But it's hard to make a promise when I am not sure what you are going to ask me."

"I need you to promise you'll hear me out. That you will listen to the whole story without reacting, or overreacting. You'll try and process what I'm telling you, and then you'll respond with your calm, clear-headedness. It's one of the things I like about you, sugar. I know you have good judgment even though you don't talk much, even though you aren't judgmental."

"Some of my exes might feel differently," he shrugged. "But I'll take it."

"Come on," said Sandy. "You know you're easy to talk to, and you know I like talking to you."

"I like talking to you too," he said.

Sandy pulled her head out of her arms and looked straight at Dusty. She looked at Dusty the way a woman looks at a man when she feels him completely, when she wants to tell him something but, more than that, needs to tell him. She looked him up and down and inside without moving her eyes from his steady gaze. Then she moved her face close to his before maneuvering her lips around the side toward his right ear saying, "And I can trust you. I know it."

She moved her face back in front of his just in time to hear him say, "You can."

She moved as close to him as she could, rubbing her left shoulder against his arm and leaning her face into his flannel shirt. He put his right arm around her and said, "Whatever it is, it will be OK. I am here for you."

She slid her right arm out across the counter and used her left hand to roll her right sleeve up to her elbow. The skin around her wrist was beautiful and fragile and she had the letters "LOVE" tattooed in cursive just past the spot where you could feel your pulse beat. As Dusty slid his eyes toward her elbow, there was the outer trace of a red circle, with the center clearly a wound, filled with some pus and beginning to scab. The symmetry of the tight circle could only lead Dusty to believe that it was a cigarette burn. Since he promised to remain calm, he took a deep breath, furrowed his brow, and pulled her close—as she whimpered softly, and tears ran down her face. Dusty didn't say a word. He just held her tight, and the tighter he held her the more easily her tears seemed to flow. She was crying into his shoulder now, and he just tried to absorb the emotions that were escaping from her body. After a few minutes, she finally said, "I … I'm sorry."

"Stop," said Dusty emphatically. "You have nothing to apologize for. Nothing."

She gathered herself together, wiped her tears, and pulled out a small mirror to look at her makeup.

"Oh, look at me," she said. "What a mess. My mascara is all over my face. Can you excuse me for a minute?"

"It's fine," said Dusty. "You don't have to go. You're … you're beautiful. You're still beautiful."

"Oh, sugar," she said. "You're so sweet. Why can't all guys be as sweet as you? That's why I call you *sugar*."

Dusty smiled. "You call everyone sugar," he said.

"Well, sugar, that may be true," said Sandy. "But, with you, I mean it."

They sat at the counter for at least fifteen minutes without saying another word. Dusty rubbed her hand on the counter and took his napkin, dipped it in ice water, and gently cleaned up the black marks on her face. She was still recovering from all of the emotions she had brought forth, and Dusty was taking this opportunity to process what he had seen in the composed manner he promised. Finally, he decided to break the ice and speak. He was careful to say what he needed to say in a steady, measured tone, without allowing his emotions to get the best of him.

"You know this ain't right?" said Dusty.

"I know, but—," she began when he cut her off.

"I'm sorry," he interjected. "But he can't do this."

"Dusty," she said, "I've called the police a half-dozen times."

"And?" said Dusty, now visibly angrier.

"Sugar, this is a small town. A small, Southern town. People know each other. People know him. The police know him. They know his family. Things are done differently here."

"Well, it ain't right," said Dusty. "It ain't goddamn right."

"It don't have to be right," said Sandy. "Some things are just the way they are."

"Why don't you leave him?" asked Dusty.

"Fear, I suppose," said Sandy. "I've wanted to leave him, tried to leave him, but I can't. I love him, or I should say I did love him. I loved him once, a long time ago, and he always says he's sorry."

"That ain't enough," said Dusty, now hotter but still under control. "It ain't near enough for you, or any woman for that matter."

"I know you're right," said Sandy. "It's just not that easy."

"You can't go back to him, Sandy," said Dusty. 'You just can't."

"I know," she said. "I know you're right, but there won't be no justice for me. Not with him. Not in this town."

Dusty stayed at the restaurant until Sandy's shift ended in the early morning. There were a couple more customers who came in to grab a bite to eat before they went to work, real early, when the sky was still dark. Sandy was glad to have Dusty there after their conversation. She was always glad to have Dusty there. He made her feel comfortable and safe, and he always listened to her. She wasn't used to men making her feel these things, and she liked the way she felt in his company. There was something so grounded about him, like he was completely at home and at ease, which seemed strange since he was still relatively new in town. But if she spent her days dreaming of running, Dusty seemed like a man who had done all the running he was ever going to do. He seemed like a man who had finally arrived at the place he was supposed to be all along.

Sandy grabbed her coat in the back and walked out from the door where employees entered and left. She was still trying to reach back for the sleeve with her left arm when Dusty came around behind her and helped slide the coat over her shoulders more easily. He pulled her close and whispered again, "It will be OK. It will all be OK."

"What are you going to say to him?" asked Sandy.

"Gonna make it clear that his days of abusing you are over."

"How will you do that?"

"Forcefully," said Dusty. "Most people don't hear messages until they are delivered in a compelling manner."

"And you know how to do that?"

"Sure," said Dusty flatly.

"How do you know?" asked Sandy, hoping for assurance.

"Years of practice," said Dusty.

* * *

"Why don't you go ahead and get in the car, Sandy," said Dusty.

"Where do you think you're going, bitch?" said Sandy's boyfriend.

"Don't pay any attention to him," said Dusty.

"She'll be back," he said. "That bitch ain't goin' nowhere."

There was a time when Dusty would have taken matters into his own hands. His bare hands. There was a time when he would have left no doubt. He would have taught Sandy's boyfriend a lesson when he was a younger man. When he was a much younger man. In those days, his instincts would have taken over, his protective instincts that could rely on his strength, his physical strength. When he could have faced the compulsion he had for fairness, and in this case, justice, head-on. When he could have stood up for Sandy in the way she deserved by enacting some degree of revenge. But those days were gone. They were long gone, and Dusty surmised it would no longer be easy to take on a younger man, and a much bigger man, at his age. It would no longer be easy, and Dusty was tired. He was so damn tired, more tired than he had ever been in his whole life. He was tired of not sleeping. Tired of acting tougher than he was. And he was tired of running. He'd just been running for so long, for as long as he could remember really, and he was tired, dead tired. He told himself this would be it. One last run. One last ride, with Sandy. He didn't know much he had left, but he knew he still had it in him. One last run, he told himself, as he stood tall in front of her young, hulking boyfriend.

"She'll be back," repeated her boyfriend. "When she gets tired of riding around with grandpa. You'll see, old man."

But Dusty didn't see. He couldn't see, and he could barely see straight. His head was spinning, and he was perspiring now. He could feel the blood running through his veins. It was warm, and it was beginning to alert his nervous system. Moreover, he didn't like being called grandpa, but he had to admit he was older, at least a heck of a lot older than Sandy's boyfriend. Age or size had never stopped him before, though. He'd fight to the death, whatever the odds, if he believed in something. Sandy was certainly worth it, but he couldn't say the same for her boyfriend. He wasn't worth getting his face beat in for, or worse, ending up in jail. In his younger years, he would never have run through these scenarios in his head. He would have reacted, swiftly and quickly and decisively.

This time, he just smiled. Despite the rush of blood that swirled inside him, Dusty had felt his legs grow weak. He had been sure not to let on, but he was unsteady, dehydrated, exhausted, and spent. His only choice was to leave, leave with Sandy, and never look back. Not for a minute.

"If I ever see you again," said Dusty, "I won't be so generous. "I'll kill you clear as day, right on the spot."

"That's funny," said her boyfriend. "Is that a promise? You've got yourself a real comedian here, Sandy. I'll be seeing you around, old man."

But Dusty wasn't listening anymore. He closed the door of the car, placed his foot to the gas, and pressed it all the way down to the floor. He sped off while still in the process of adjusting his seatbelt. Sandy was crying, but she linked her arms around his right arm as he used his right hand to shift into third gear.

Dusty had run before. He had run plenty of times. Out of Texas. Across the Southwest. Through parts of California. And most recently from Nevada. But he had always run alone. Just him. No extra baggage and no one else to consider. Quick and easy. Just get up and go. He never had to think. He just did it. No questions asked. And it was often his own livelihood that was at stake.

This was different. Nobody was chasing him. Not really. Heck, Sandy's boyfriend didn't even stand up. He'd probably go after Sandy at some point, but not before he was sure she wasn't coming back. He was calling her bluff now, and he never believed she'd go through with it.

No, this was different, and it felt different. Dusty had played a role in helping Sandy make a break, and he felt a sense of responsibility. This made him think harder about each decision. Where would they go next? He had more than just himself to think about now. This frightened him. It frightened him to think about Sandy, to know that she was counting on him, but he liked it too. He liked that she was counting on him. And he had to come through for her. After all, she deserved it.

They sped out of the neighborhood, and he merged the car onto the nearest freeway.

"Well," said Dusty. "You're free now. He'll never touch you again."

As they pulled out onto the road and headed for the highway, he looked over at Sandy. She had been through a lot, but she had so much life ahead of her. He had so much less, and he felt the fatigue of his years crawling over him. He was sweating more now, almost as if his insides were now processing everything that had just occurred during the confrontation with her boyfriend. Even though Dusty didn't sleep well, he rarely felt tired. But he felt tired now, as tired as he'd ever felt in his whole life. Tired of everything, but tired of running most of all. He had finally arrived at a place he didn't have to run from, didn't want to run from, and here he was ... running. There was no choice now. Running was what he had to do, even if he was doubting his ability to do it.

Dusty was pedaling that Buick down the freeway when it hit him that this decision had been made in a matter of seconds. Decisions like this usually are. He was no stranger to these types of moments, but Sandy, well, she was different. She'd lived her whole life in South Carolina and only left the state once—when she went to Florida with her girlfriends. Her whole life was in that town. It's where she was raised, and it was the only place she had ever called home. Her boyfriend was the sonofabitch. Why should she have to be the one to leave?

He looked over at her in the passenger seat. She was so young, so impossibly young. When Dusty looked at her, he could see a life even she couldn't imagine when she looked in the mirror. That's what time does for you. What experience does for you. It opens your eyes, allows you to predict things more accurately, even if it ruins the plot before you've actually seen the movie. And that's what Dusty could see, and what he knew Sandy didn't know. He could see her life and her family and her friends. It was all there. It was all still there. Those things would be little more than memories wherever they were heading. Sure, she'd be miles away from her boyfriend, but not everyone is meant for the road. Not everyone is meant to abandon all they've known, all that's come before. It's not an easy thing to do, but it's the reality once the veneer of the honeymoon wears off. One day, you just wake up in bed, roll over, and realize you are somewhere else, somewhere different, and that the only chance at happiness is to become someone else. That's not for everyone, and Dusty couldn't be sure it was for Sandy.

Beyond that, how could he even know, truly know, that he was the man for Sandy? Sure, he fantasized a bit about them being together. They had a connection, a real connection, on an emotional level. But they had never once been together, not physically anyway. They hadn't even shared a kiss. At the same time, he knew what they shared was genuine and true, in part because it was not physical. It hadn't been that way with his ex-wives. Not even close. It was the physical attraction that had come first. With Sandy, he felt at ease just hearing the sweet sound of her voice, the way it traveled across the air with that easy drawl and made it seem like everything would be alright.

He just wondered if he was being selfish, but he knew that he'd never find another woman like Sandy. He'd been around, and he knew this. He knew it deep in his core, and he felt it every time she called him "sugar" or threw her head back at one of his jokes, and he felt it when she leaned in with her arms hooked through his or cried on his shoulder. A heart like hers didn't come along often, and it was worth protecting. Worth fighting for. Still, deep down, he knew she deserved someone better. Better than him, with less mileage, fewer skeletons, and more impossible hopes. More unimaginable optimism.

He tried to flush these thoughts out of his head and focus on the road. He just kept driving. Blindly. Driving without a plan or destination. With each mile marker, it seemed that Sandy was beginning to breathe easier. She had wiped her tears a time or two and was sitting up now. The middle of the day was bright, and she put her sunglasses on and leaned her head back against the headrest of the passenger seat. She rolled the window down, stuck her arm out, and let her face feel the wind.

Dusty had worked in a casino, but he'd never felt like a lucky man. No, he'd never felt lucky. Not ever. But he felt lucky now. He felt genuinely lucky for the first time in his life. He wasn't sure he deserved it, that he was worthy of it, but he felt it. Good fortune is supposed to arrive at the doors of those who have earned it, he thought, and he couldn't be sure that he had. Sandy, on the other hand, was good to the core. She didn't have a bad bone in her body. The goodness ran right through her, and he felt it the first time he met her at the Waffle House. He wouldn't go as far as to say it was love at first sight, but he knew she was unlike any woman he had met before, that she could never be capable of having an agenda, of being anything other than the warm, sweet soul she was. It was a gift, as rare and unique and powerful as the gift of an exceptional athlete or a brilliant mathematician. Dusty didn't know if everyone could see it, but he could. It made him feel good to know that he could see it.

"Where do you want to go, Sandy?" said Dusty.

"Shh …," whispered Sandy. "Just drive, sugar."

They were heading south on 85. They'd cross the Georgia line soon. They could cut down to New Orleans and listen to some jazz, thought Dusty. Or they could just head to Houston. Sandy would look great in a cowboy hat, he bet. If they wanted, they could cross the border in Laredo and head south into Mexico. The drug trade was raging there, but the beaches were still beautiful, and the drinks ran colder there. He could use a drink, he thought, to clear his head if nothing else. He was thinking for both of them, or trying to, and for the first time in his life, he felt uncertain, unclear. Oh, he'd made poor decisions before, but he'd always been certain of them at the time. He'd never doubted or wondered or debated with himself in the moment. Later, maybe, but not in the moment. Sandy was so young, but she was already wise. Wiser than he was. He knew she was wise, and despite her youth, Dusty knew he'd follow her anywhere. It might have been selfish, but he knew he'd be OK if they were together. He was always OK when they were together. And she would be too, just as long as they were together. He didn't want to possess her or control her or define her or decide for her. But he knew he wanted to be near her. He wanted to be by her side, to lay down next to her at the end of every day from that moment forward. He didn't want anything in the world other than to be close enough to avoid the red glare of the sun in the coolness her shadow.

"Sugar," she said, smiling, as the wind whipped through her yellow hair. "Just drive. We'll know where we're going just as soon as we get there."

HIGHWAY 5

Whenever Roland Mathews drove on the 5 Freeway in California, he thought of that day, five years before, when he had seen something terrible. The memories were worse when he was coming off a migraine, with his senses slightly dulled and more susceptible to summoning the images of that afternoon. It was a day he would much rather have forgotten, but some days it felt as if it had happened yesterday.

He had never thought about the possibility of a day like this when he became a trucker. Roland had served his country with distinction and been in wars in the Middle East. He understood the finality of a battlefield. He was well aware of what was at stake, and he knew what it meant to see more than you bargained for. But driving a truck was supposed to provide some relief and ease him back into society. He hoped it would provide a reflective outlet for him to decompress, an outlet that arrived day after day with an endless supply of roads.

Roland always liked the road. He enjoyed family car trips as a kid, and his fascination with the road continued into adulthood. The older he got, the more he liked being on the road alone. There was something comforting about it. It seemed to go on forever. It was peaceful, and it offered him time. The road wasn't a place to be in a hurry. It was a place to savor—even more so after his tours of duty were over. Now was the time for something different. Slow time and time alone were what he wanted more than anything.

Overseas, it was just the opposite. When you are at war, time is all you have until you have none. At those moments, there isn't time to do anything but react, using a combination of instincts and training in hopes you'll make the right decision. More often than not, Roland's judgment was good, but he was glad not to be forced into those situations anymore, where someone's life depended on what he did or didn't do in a split second.

Out on the open road, sitting up high in his comfortable cab, he still needed to be attentive. A car could make a sudden move, after all. But he wasn't on high alert, not like he was when he navigated land mines in the desert. Roland drove with a modicum of calm, and this provided him with an existence where he could relax and let his mind contemplate what his existence had become.

Roland often thought of his wife and his children. He had left them behind when he went off to war, and he had hoped they would be there for him when he returned. They were. What he didn't count on was that he was the one who had changed, and he no longer seemed equipped to integrate back into the life he had departed.

Being on the road allowed him to live that life in doses. It wasn't like going off to war, but it allowed him to digest his domestic reality in smaller segments. He could compartmentalize it when he was home, knowing he would be on the road before too long. Although he felt guilty about his limited tolerance for family life, the war had altered his chemistry. It had made him more cynical, impatient, and ill-tempered. It was his hope that life on the road might gradually return his psyche to a less restless place.

One afternoon in late March, Roland was driving back from Redding, California, heading south on the 5 Freeway. Although the 5 runs through some of the biggest metropolitan areas on the West Coast, it also goes on for huge stretches of time where the landscape is bare and desolate. Roland liked these long, desolate portions of the road. They reminded him, in some ways, of the desert in the Middle East. There was something spare and vacant that was familiar, and Roland could embrace that. But he also knew the hours out here could swallow you whole if you weren't careful.

Roland was in the right lane when a minivan passed him with a full car. It was comprised of a large family, perhaps on their way back from a weekend camping up near Mount Shasta or in the Redwoods. It looked like the father was driving, and the kids in the back peered out the window and motioned for him to honk his horn. He didn't see kids do this much these days, but he remembered sitting in the back seat with his brother and doing this all the time when they were kids. That seemed like a simpler time and thinking of those days made him smile. He gave the kids an enthusiastic honk, and they smiled in approval before the minivan disappeared into the distance ahead of him.

Nearly a half hour later, the cars ahead of him began to slow rapidly. He pressed the brakes of his cab and could smell the smell of burnt tires as he brought the hulking tons of metal to a complete stop only to see something so unreal that his eyes were hardly equipped to process it.

Across the median, the minivan was lying upside down, its wheels still spinning, as smoke poured through the car and out from the chassis of the mangled vehicle. The sheet metal of the minivan had been altered irrevocably, the result of what could only have been a tremendous impact. About twenty feet away, there was an 18-wheeler with steam pouring out of its cab. Roland watched the driver push the door open slowly and stumble out of the vehicle before getting himself out of harm's way at the side of the road. He was bleeding from his head, but he appeared to have escaped without more serious injuries.

Roland then turned his attention to the median. There, beneath the warm California sun, atop a soft bed of grass, were the catastrophic remnants of the accident. In some ways, the horrors exceeded what the trucker had witnessed during his time on the battlefield, since they included the broken bodies of children. Roland put his hand over his mouth and threw up on the floor mat in front of the driver's seat.

After a few seconds to gather himself, Roland pulled his truck to the side of the highway and rushed toward the accident in hopes of finding any survivors from the crash.

He could feel the chemistry change inside his body. His blood ran colder, and he transitioned to the once-familiar sensation of a soldier standing amidst bodies on the battlefield. Someone else had already called 911, but the ambulances and police cars had yet to arrive on the scene.

It was difficult to tell exactly what had occurred, but it seemed most likely that the minivan had a tire blow, which sent the vehicle hurtling out of control through the median and into oncoming traffic, where it met its fate with a massive 18-wheeler. The force of the collision was so great that a number of passengers had been thrown from the vehicle—including the children in the back who the trucker had seen less than an hour before.

The accident was not survivable, and all that was left was the carnage. Blood on the windshield and steering wheel, across the pavement, and the torn bodies that only minutes before carried so much life. It was clear their souls had now left this world, and the trucker knew what to do in this situation. He wished he didn't know, but he did. He had done it before, and he acted swiftly and calmly while passing cars looked on in disbelief.

Although Roland probably should have waited for the police to arrive, he couldn't bear to see the bodies contorted and strewn across the terrain. He picked each one up with the utmost care and then carried them to a soft patch of grass where he could set them down peacefully alongside one another. He felt they deserved to be together and to have their bodies well cared for at the very least.

Roland then remembered that he had some extra sheets in the back of his truck, and he rushed to get them even though life had already passed through the bodies he had lined so tenderly in the grass. Still, they didn't deserve to be looked upon, not by cars passing by, not by him, not by anyone, not in this way, in this place.

Cover the dead. It's all he could think about, just as he did when men who had fought beside him in combat were lying on the battlefield. For God's sake, cover the dead.

THE BORDER

Jorge Sanchez had worked along the border for many years. He had worked beneath the great sky, perspiring in the warm California sun.

This wasn't just any border. This was the border of the United States of America, the southern border, near San Diego. This particular crossing provided unique challenges, and it was a difficult job. From the twenty-somethings who headed to the Baja beaches in search of cheap hotels and partying to the working poor who traveled to Tijuana for cheaper medicines, this revolving door was an active gateway that perpetually linked Mexico and the United States.

Working along the border required cooperation between law enforcement officials of both countries. Payoffs and bribes weren't uncommon, and you could never really be sure of who was on your side or any side for that matter. It wasn't easy to determine whether or not you were being played or where loyalties lay, and you had to watch your own back before you could turn your attention to someone else's. Standing post in a uniform along the line tested morals like few occupations.

The public's perception was that the Mexican border was America's link to a seedier world—where drug lords reigned supreme and crooked cops came by the dozen. The United States had long pledged its commitment to fighting "the war on drugs" with the help of more secure borders. This played best with White voters, many of whom were already afraid of Mexico. These fears, embedded in dangerous stereotypes, ranged from the possibility of being kidnapped on vacation in Acapulco to Mexican gangs infiltrating the US. For some, it was no more complicated than the simple fact that both legal and illegal immigrants were taking more and more jobs, that the country was becoming more diverse each year. Although many people saw this as progress, there were always going to be some who wished they could go back in time. People pouring in from the southern border made that impossible. Although some of these fears weren't entirely unfounded, the media also had a hand in crafting these narratives.

Still, the United States had long played the role of Puritan victim, whose pristine land had been infiltrated by illegal substances despite their best efforts to curtail the flow back and forth. This narrative was equally naive, and anyone who truly believed the United States was completely innocent was only seeing what they wanted to see. After all, the US was the most powerful country on earth, and other countries didn't impose their will if it wasn't welcomed, perhaps not publicly, but rather behind the curtains where the strings were pulled. The truth is the demand for drugs was extraordinarily high in the United States, and cartels in Mexico (and Colombia) capitalized on it. Powerful people on both sides turned it into big business.

Of course, the border agents knew these harsh realities, but few allowed themselves to admit it, even privately. Jorge was no exception. This was more a function of self-preservation than naivety. After all, if you were going to stand watch and patrol the border, armed and ready, it was important to be able to justify your existence, to make sense of all the hours you spent along the line. It was too dangerous and too stressful not to convince yourself that there were two very distinct sides here, and that you stood on the side of righteousness.

Even if this was necessary, Jorge knew the world was not black and white, that it couldn't be distilled down to good and evil or right and wrong. Nothing was that simple. And certainly not the border. Jorge had always known this, and he approached his job with a conscious detachment that was different from many of his colleagues. He wasn't ever going to allow himself to be caught up in the "nobility" of it all, and the best he could aspire to was to conduct his work with a professionalism and precision that provided Jorge with the type of clarity the job itself did not. There was no room for sentimentality, emotion, and most of all, the kind of arrogant American exceptionalism that bought into hierarchy as a birthright.

The job of a border patrol agent was also different as a Mexican American, if only because of the manner in which coworkers perceived their peers with Mexican blood. Many of Jorge's coworkers assumed he would be more lenient on Mexicans trying to enter the United States, that he would be more susceptible to bribes, that he was somehow less American than they were. Jorge could feel their suspicious eyes on him nearly all the time. From the beginning, he could sense their mistrust.

In Jorge's case, he had grown up in the United States, in El Paso, an infamous border town in its own right, but he was American. This was the only country he had ever known. Still, being of Mexican heritage was a source of great pride. Jorge traveled to Mexico with his family to visit relatives far from the border in Oaxaca. He embraced his family's roots, their traditions, and the Spanish language. It was a central part of his character.

Oaxaca was a special place to Jorge, in part due to its natural beauty but more so due to the taste of the food his grandmother prepared in her kitchen and served at her modest, wooden dining table. Even though she passed away years ago, he could still smell the spices that wafted through the air above her stove. Her enchiladas *con mole negro* were as fresh in his mind as the first day he had tasted them, on a trip as a nine-year-old boy. He remembered her words as he sat across from her at the table. *"Jorge,"* she said. *"Just because we don't have electricity in this house doesn't mean we are in the dark."* Since he could barely see the food in front of him, this made little sense at the time, but as he got older, the wisdom of his *abuela* helped him navigate the complexities of life.

At the same time, Jorge was always happy to return to the United States after these visits. Despite his family's origins, he was an American kid, with American things and American friends and, most of all, American ideals. This was the land of the free, as his parents had reiterated to him. And while they didn't use the phrase *American Dream* in the traditional sense, they liked to tell Jorge that everyone could have a dream in America. Dreams, however farfetched they might be, were very important, and Jorge could dream here. For his relatives in Mexico, this wasn't always the case. His grandmother would tell him, *"Dreams are more important than reality. For reality will always be there, but dreams come and go like the wind."* Jorge understood this. *"Fulfilling a dream,"* she would add, *"is far less important than having one."*

But he didn't dream of being a border agent. Like most American kids, he dreamed of something more glamorous, more prosperous. If pressed, he'd say he wanted to be a professional baseball player. Baseball was a sport that was embedded in both Mexican and American culture, and he played in the streets with his friends as a boy every chance he got. When the Los Angeles Dodgers brought Fernando Valenzuela over from Mexico, the eyes of every Mexican American were squarely upon him. Jorge was no different. As fame and fortune and adulation descended upon Valenzuela in America, Jorge dreamed of millions of people one day knowing his name. But his grandmother cautioned against this. *"It is better to be respected by those who are worthy than adored by those who are not,"* she said.

But seeing Valenzuela, a Mexican, on the mound, his blue and white jersey pulled over his round belly, was a genuine thrill for Jorge that went beyond his popularity. Valenzuela was strangely compelling. His childlike smile. His charming broken English. And his unorthodox delivery—where he rolled his eyes back, tilted his head to the sky, and somehow seemed to summon the heavens. More than anything, though, Fernando Valenzuela's success in America allowed Mexican American kids to dream of being something more. Something more than they imagined. More than their parents. Jorge's grandmother could see his enthusiasm, and she didn't want to thwart it. But she was always keeping him grounded. *"Remember, Jorge,"* she said. *"Just because you want to be something more doesn't mean your parents are something less."*

The border may not have been a calling for Jorge, but duty was. His sense of duty led him to enlist in the Marines, and he did two tours in the Middle East. War wasn't what he expected. The desert was blazing hot, and the enemy couldn't always be seen. They had to watch out for land mines nearly every step they took. But at least they knew who the enemy was, even if they couldn't always see them. Having a clear idea of the enemy was vitally important. It provided a clarity of purpose that was difficult to obtain working on the border when he returned home from the war.

The daylight hours on the border were somewhat straightforward. The long lines of cars in both directions. Miles of fencing along sparse landscapes. People waiting. Passports and paperwork. It all made sense, more or less. Of course, there was the chance of hiding in plain sight, but vision afforded Jorge a feeling of certainty that was missing when the sun went down. His grandmother felt differently. She used to say, *"Uncertainty exists, not so much to make us uneasy, but rather to remind us that we are alive."*

The nights reminded him that he was alive but also of his time in the Marines. The eerie quiet, along with the knowledge that countless tunnels existed beneath their feet while they worked amidst the silence. *"Sometimes a world without sound,"* his grandmother would say, *"can speak volumes inside our own heads."* She was right, of course. Jorge tried to tune his ears to the quiet in order to attend to his duties. After all, he had to be ready for those travelers who might be trying to cross over into the United States. Jorge often felt terribly alone at night, working in the invisible darkness but always with the eyes of the world gazing down upon him.

Although he was too young to remember it, Jorge still had a scar on the lower part of his left leg where the fence had cut him as a small boy when his parents pulled him underneath the metal wiring and into America on a cool autumn night. The scar served as a constant reminder of the manner in which he came to this country, and there was a painful irony that he was now charged with ensuring others couldn't do the same.

He was just lucky, he thought. Lucky he made it into this country and even luckier that the Immigration Control and Reform Act of 1986 legalized illegal immigrants who had arrived in the United States prior to 1982. Jorge and his family had the good fortune of being able to take advantage of this law. Families with similar hopes and dreams today didn't have the same luxury, but that didn't keep them from trying to cross, from risking their lives (and the lives of their children) in search of better ones. Perhaps this was Jorge's penance, now tasked with keeping these families from the chance of realizing their dreams the way he did. The nights brought all of these thoughts to the forefront of Jorge's mind in moments of stillness, and he was once again reminded of his grandma's words. *"Jorge, you don't need light to be able to see,"* she seemed to whisper to him in the dark, quiet air.

He wasn't the president. He wasn't a congressman. Or a judge. He was just a man. A man stationed along the border. He didn't make these laws. He only promised to enforce them, after he had fought in wars to protect them. But he also had Mexican blood that ran through his veins. Mexican American blood. And these weren't drug traffickers, rapists, or hardened criminals. They were just families. Families. Mothers and fathers pinning their hopes on coming across a border agent like Jorge, in the dead of night, holding their children in their arms with the eyes of the world overhead, pleading for one chance to be Jorge Sanchez or Fernando Valenzuela.

HENRY AND THE COWBOY

We pulled into the parking lot early in the morning. The sun was just coming up over the plains, and we would never have known the steel mill had closed down just by looking at the sky beginning to take on light. We turned the motor off and twisted the key backward, so we could listen to the radio. It used a little bit of battery power to do this, but we weren't going to be in the car for too long. Once we saw the lights come on inside the restaurant, we would turn off the electricity in the car and get something to eat.

While we sat inside the car, with the windows up, we noticed that we were not alone. There was an oversized man in his forties standing three spaces down from us. He had no vehicle and was standing in the center of the parking space. He was a big man, and he took up nearly as much space as a small car, but he was just standing there, with his belly protruding over his waist and his brown leather shoes pointed toward the dark windows of the restaurant. The man had thick, Coke-bottle glasses, and he wiped them off with his thumb before readjusting them on his wide face. He wore brown slacks and a dark jacket that fit his overweight body poorly.

I leaned back in my seat as John fiddled with the radio. It wasn't easy to find good music on at this time in the morning, and sports talk radio wasn't as good as during the workweek—when people were stuck in traffic on the way to the office. John kept hitting the seek button over and over until he stumbled onto a channel that played some old Motown hits. Music from Motown seemed to go better with the night than the morning, but the sky was still a bit dark, and we sat there and listened to Smokey Robinson and Martha and the Vandellas before the day took shape. John liked newer music more, but even he had to admit these songs were good. "There is something in the sound of Motown that never lets you get too sad, even when they are singing about sad things," he said.

It was true. The Motown era had an indomitable spirit that could carry you through the dark and the light.

It might have been intended to be heard at nighttime, but the sounds extended beyond that and permeated their way into our consciousness. They seemed to be tinged with more than a touch of hope, regardless of the situation, and they made me feel better about the future even though they were written in the past. It made me think of this town and the steel mill that had closed. Many of the folks who worked there were now unemployed, and the area would have to reinvent itself. That wouldn't be easy but, sitting in the car, listening to Motown made me think that, somehow, they would find a way. People would find a way. They always do. A way to keep going, through the darkness, until they appeared on the other side and the light shone on their shoulders once again. I didn't know how they would do this when everything seemed so bleak, but the Temptations assured me they would find a way, that I shouldn't doubt the resilience of the human spirit even in times like this, especially in times like this.

Just then, the lights inside the restaurant went on, and a young man in a uniform walked to the glass doors to unlock them. The man in the parking space saw him before we did and, despite the size of his frame, began moving forcefully, rapidly, making a beeline for the glass doors. He walked aggressively and awkwardly, somewhat like those strange people you sometimes see speed walking in the neighborhood, his arms swinging back and forth at his sides.

When he finally made it to the door, he flung it open with such force that it was nearly enough to overpower the spring. He leaned back, so the door would not hit him when he pulled it open, and then he entered the restaurant. We followed him into the restaurant at half the speed only to find him waiting patiently behind the Please Wait to Be Seated sign when we arrived. We stood a few feet behind him to give him his space after his strong move to get inside the restaurant.

The inside of the building had more character than the outside. The interior had the feel of one of those old restaurants you might find on a country road, emerging out of the dark like a beacon, with the smell of food spilling onto the roadside. It was a real joint, a classic diner, with lots of aluminum, the requisite fluorescent lighting, and the ever-important kitchen window that allowed cooks to toss plates of food up onto a counter and ring a bell signifying orders were ready. They had just turned on the griddle, and the place already smelled of grease. The booths were all covered in pleather that was durable and could be wiped down easily, and it even possessed an old-school counter with easy moving, round barstools with O-shaped backs that were once so popular. While we weren't sure it would pass every health inspector's standards, we felt pretty confident the food was going to be good.

The man who opened the door led the large man to a booth on the right just past the counter and then returned to seat us in the booth behind him. This was done to make the job of the servers easier, with tables of people clustered together so they could move quickly from one to another.

A waitress appeared in a blue dress and dropped off two menus on our table. She must have entered from the back, since we didn't see her walk in the front door. She was average height and lean, with a kind face and light brown hair that swooped down the back of her neck and across her shoulders. We just caught a glimpse of her name tag that had the letters "FLO" printed on the hard plastic.

It was hard to believe her name was really Flo. That name felt fictitious, since it went out of style years ago. Perhaps she just had a wry sense of humor, wanted older customers to feel a bit of nostalgia or, more likely, wanted to maintain the anonymity of her real identity. Of course, it was possible that her parents had given her that name. But that seemed unlikely. Wholly unlikely. Plus, there was no better way to keep her real name a secret than to have a name tag emblazoned with those three iconic, generic letters. Either way, we thought it was cool.

Just then, another man, quite a bit older, walked into the restaurant and made his way to the table with the large man who had been waiting in the parking lot. He was in his seventies and quite lean for his age. He had white hair and a tanned face, and his toes pointed slightly outward when he walked. There was something strange and unconventional about him.

He sat down across from the man from the parking spot without either of them saying a word. It was clear they had arranged to have breakfast today even if their relationship wasn't built on verbal communication. The older man had an almost blank smile pasted across his face, and his eyes danced as he looked at the menu gleefully. The waitress came over to pour him a cup of coffee.

"Morning, Flo!" he said.

"Hi, Henry," said Flo in a warm, if somewhat reluctant, manner that let us know he was a regular.

"Last night, I had a dream," said Henry. "Cowboys in white suits!"

"Wow," said Flo, doing a pretty credible job of feigning genuine excitement. "Cowboys, Henry! In white suits no less! How exciting."

"Yes, it's true," Henry responded enthusiastically. "They were riding on their horses, all through the city filled with cars."

"That's really something," said Flo. "What'll it be, Henry? The usual?"

Henry nodded, smiling.

"And you, Wyatt?" she said turning to the big man, who pointed to three different selections on the menu, one after another, without saying a word.

"Alrighty," said Flo, as she scribbled their orders on the ticket and casually moved to our booth to take our orders.

"Hi y'all doin'?" she said in a friendly, unaffected manner. "What can I get you?"

"I'll have the pancakes," said John. "With hash browns and bacon."

Flo wrote this casually on the notepad. "And you?" she inquired, turning in my direction.

"I am going to have the Denver omelet," I announced, "With Swiss cheese, hash browns, and sausages along with a side of white toast."

She added my order to the list and let us know that it would be "right up" before attaching our order, along with the order from the table next to ours, up on a wire for the cook to read.

I looked over at the two men sitting at the table next to us. The man Flo had referred to as Wyatt unbuttoned his jacket. All this time, he had been sitting in the booth with his jacket still on and zipped all the way to the top. When he removed it, he revealed one of those country-and-western shirts with a stitched design as well as a thin bolo tie down the front. To top it off, he wore a silver star on his left breast that glistened under the fluorescent lights as if it had been recently polished.

Flo swung back by our tables with coffees for the two of us, along with a couple of glasses of orange juice for Henry and Wyatt.

"Flo," Henry called out to her. "Did you know Wyatt here used to be a cowboy?"

"Yes," she remarked. "You told me that, Henry."

"It's true," said Henry. "Used to ride a horse and everything. Even carried a revolver! Six-shooter, right?" said Henry, turning toward Wyatt.

Wyatt put down his orange juice and nodded before returning to take another sip out of the straw.

"That's amazing," said Flo, happily playing along in a manner that told us this she was familiar with this routine. And not just familiar but patient. Patient and kind. "You must have been very brave, Wyatt," said Flo.

Wyatt remained timid, inward, unable to lift his head all the way up, but he did manage to tip his hat to Flo, which was clearly a meaningful acknowledgment.

The cook rang the bell, and Flo went back to the kitchen and grabbed all the plates she could. It was impressive that she was able to carry so many at one time.

John and I ate our breakfasts eagerly. The food tasted good. There is something about eating breakfast in the morning when the sky is still dark that seems to make food taste better. It was still very early in the morning, and we were the only customers in the restaurant along with the two gentlemen in the booth beside us.

Flo was very attentive. She came by to ask if there was anything else we needed. I was all set, but John asked for hot sauce, which Flo got for him. He always liked to put hot sauce on his hash browns, and Flo said not many people did that. Once we were taken care of, she sat down at the table next to us and said, "Henry, you were telling me about the cowboys in white suits."

Henry's eyes lit up. She really was kind, and for a moment I wondered if her presence there had been preordained, like some kind of earth angel that was in this particular place for this particular reason. It really was something. Henry smiled excitedly and then stuttered over his breath a bit eagerly trying to get the next words out now that Flo was sitting at their table. Wyatt just kept eating and didn't say a word.

"Well," said Henry. "The cowboys with white suits were riding down the street."

"Yes …," Flo said and smiled, seeming to show genuine interest now.

"Kids ran out to see the cowboys," exclaimed Henry. "And the cowboys twirled their six-shooters for them."

"The kids must have loved that," added Flo.

"They did," said Henry. "And they loved their white suits. But just then, the cowboys learned there were bad men in town."

"Oh no," said Flo.

"The bad men were at the saloon bothering the townspeople, so the cowboys rode over, in their white suits, and ran the bad men off."

"I am so glad," exclaimed Flo, relieved.

"But now the cowboys were hungry," said Henry. "So, they returned to the saloon and had breakfast."

A few people had now entered the restaurant and were waiting to be seated, just as we finished eating. They were lined up just inside the door. Flo looked over and saw she had more customers waiting to be served, but she wanted to make sure that Henry had the chance to finish his story and the other customers would have to wait.

"I like cowboys, Henry," said Flo. "And I like the cowboys in white suits. I like them very much."

"You know," said Henry, "Wyatt used to be one."

TRAVIS

Travis was the first one I knew to get a fake ID. I thought it was pretty cool. He looked old anyway, and now he was old. At least on paper. He was also from California, because the California ID was easy to duplicate back then, and nobody in the South had ever seen one before.

When he first got it made, I looked at the ID carefully. It was his picture to be sure, and the laminate was better than average. There were no rough edges around the outside, and this was in the days before holograms complicated things. Sure, it was possible that someone might have wondered if it was a fake. But store owners in South Carolina had nothing to compare it to. There weren't a lot of Californians in South Carolina to begin with, and so Travis didn't have much trouble using the ID effectively.

Travis was one year older than me. He was taller than most, having gone through puberty earlier than the rest of us. Perhaps he was older than we thought. He moved here when he was fifteen, or so he said, and some people wondered if he had been held back in school. Either way, his face was more hardened. It wore the pain of experience, and it sprouted out from the stubble of his goatee and laced his animal eyes with something wild that told us Travis knew what it meant to be savage in a way that we did not.

Even so, Travis was cool, impossibly cool, and I was drawn to him. It didn't matter that I was a good kid, and it was of little consequence that I knew he was the wrong crowd. I knew better, but Travis had a magnetism that was compelling. Furthermore, I didn't have many friends. I was shy, like many teenagers, and kids my age were merciless. They never missed a chance to remind me that I was a virgin or that I had never had a girlfriend. It wasn't as if I really longed to be like them. I just longed to be normal or at least not teased for being different. And Travis never teased me. Not once.

The first day I met him he said, "Hey, I'm Travis," before adding, "don't pay any attention to them. They're idiots."

Even though Travis didn't hang out with that crowd, he had their respect. This was because he struck a healthy amount of fear in them. Everything about him made people uncomfortable. It oozed from his giant, gold belt buckle to his leather boots. When his eyes narrowed someone in their gaze, they were genuinely afraid—not of being assaulted with words but of something worse, something unpredictable. I don't like to use the word crazy, but Travis possessed an internal wildness, and the kids who teased me were never going to mess with Travis. And from the day he came to our school, they stopped messing with me. That was more than anyone else had ever done for me, and so, when Travis called to me after school and said, "Let's go," I went.

It was almost summer, and the day was impossibly hot. The air in South Carolina can be stifling, and, on that afternoon, you could have cut it with a knife. I began perspiring the moment I walked out of the brick building and stepped into the moist air. Travis seemed almost impervious to sweat, even in jeans, and he was waiting outside in front of the school.

Travis drove an old Chevy pickup. It had a manual transmission, and there was a touch of rust coming through the body. But the engine was strong. It had been rebuilt by Travis and his uncle, and it started up easily as we pulled away from the school. It was a Friday. Friday afternoon. The end of the school week. No homework to be completed for the next day, and a sense that anything teachers had assigned could wait, would have to wait, at least until later in the weekend. This provided Friday with a sense of unbridled freedom that wasn't felt on any other day of the week. I had the feeling that every day felt like this for Travis, but Fridays felt different for me.

We rolled the windows down and drove out past the city limits. We lived in a city that was hardly modern, but it had a degree of order. It was, at the very least, civilized, and people were relatively educated too, since it had a university. When you got outside of town, things slowly began to change. The grass grew taller. Buildings were further apart, and there was an unspoken feeling that, out there, law and order was placed in the hands of the people. If the stereotype of a "country boy" was born anywhere, it might as well have been there.

We pulled into the driveway of a convenience store and parked over the cracked cement. Travis went inside and grabbed a case of beer. I grabbed a soda, and we placed the beverages on the counter. The man looked at Travis a bit suspiciously and inquired, "You twenty-one, boy?"

"Yes, sir," said Travis.

"Let me see some ID, please," said the man behind the counter. He didn't say it skeptically so much as to keep Travis honest. After all, his face looked every bit of twenty-one, even if his body still looked like a long, wiry teen.

"Here you go, sir," said Travis, while the man eyed the license as if he had never seen one from California before. Travis sensed this and interacted smartly, "Just moved back here with my mom from California. I was born here, and it's good to be back in the South."

The man behind the counter seemed to like Travis's comment and his effect. He came across like a true Southerner, a young good ole boy in many ways, and the man behind the counter was convinced even if he added, "Providing alcohol to a minor is illegal," as he peered in my direction while I held my Pepsi.

"Of course, sir," said Travis. "We are just having a few people over, and my mom and my uncle will be there. Just a small gathering. We'll keep an eye on my cousin, here."

I couldn't lie to anyone. I would have started sweating and crumbled instantly. And I marveled at how cool Travis was. He was so poised that it almost didn't seem like a lie. It was as if we had become these other people, as if I had become something else, someone else, in that small window of time since we left the school.

We hopped back in the car and drove out to the lake. The lake was something I knew very little about. It had a mythical quality to it, and it possessed a forbidden element that had an allure for any teenager. I heard stories, but I had never been there, save for the time I went with my parents when I was a little kid, and that didn't count.

Travis turned off the main road. "Almost there," he said. The surface of the road now changed to gravel, and there were tall trees on both sides. It had been a wet spring, and the whole area was very green. Driving away from the main road, it nearly felt like we could be engulfed, almost inhaled into the wilderness. But it was unquestionably beautiful there.

Travis passed the main campground and picnic area and drove around to the other side of the lake. He turned down another road that wasn't much more than a wide trail and steered his old pickup between the narrow trees like he had done this before. There was a small space to pull off to the side, almost like a parking space made by vehicles that had parked there repeatedly in the past. Travis turned the wheel to the right, squeezed in between two trunks, and threw the truck into park. We hopped out of the truck, grabbed our backpacks, and I followed Travis down a trail that led away from the lake.

We hiked for about twenty minutes until we could hear running water. Then we stepped off the trail and cut down to the riverbed, where there was a nice creek with a secluded swimming hole. The air was still hot and wet and muggy, and a swim in the afternoon heat sounded good. There were two girls there, and they were sitting on a towel in the sun atop a rock along the creek. When they heard us, they turned their heads, and one of the girls nodded to Travis as if she knew him.

"Hey, Janie," called Travis.

"Travis," she said in an unsurprised way that let me know they had planned to meet us at this spot. "You're late."

"Traffic," Travis deadpanned, which was as close to a joke as he could muster.

Janie was tall and lean and tanned with shoulder-length brown hair that she wore beneath a baseball cap that was nearly pulled down over her eyes. She wore cut-off jeans that revealed all they could. Her long, browned legs seemed to go on for miles, and she wasn't wearing shoes. She had a wide mouth with full lips, and she partially revealed her breasts from beneath her Allman Brothers tank top.

We walked over to them, and Travis leaned in and gave Janie a kiss in a way that showed neither embarrassment nor overzealousness—just a confidence and poise I had only seen before in the movies.

"I'm Kyle," I interjected awkwardly into the silence that hung in the air after their kiss.

"Hey, Kyle," said Janie flatly. "I'm Janie, and this is my cousin Talia."

Talia smiled shyly but didn't say a word. She didn't possess any of the sheer confidence that Janie exhibited, but her smile was welcoming. Like Janie, she wore cut-off shorts, but they weren't cut nearly as low and looked as if they might have been turned into shorts just recently. She had a white summer blouse with buttons that ran straight down the center. Her hair was sandy brown, bone straight, and she wore it pulled back in a ponytail.

Travis grabbed Janie's hand and said, "Come on!" and they both got up from the large rock and headed toward the water hole. I sat down next to Talia and said nothing as we watched Travis and Janie take off their clothes and plunge themselves into the water unabashedly. Janie jumped on Travis's back and reached her arms around his neck while he swam away from us carrying both of them. Now at the far end of the swimming hole, we saw Janie kiss the back of Travis's neck and swing her body around to embrace him face-to-face.

"Want to take a walk?" I said to Talia.

"Sure. OK," said Talia, not so much cautious as slightly indifferent. After all, we had barely met and didn't know each other at all. Still, there was a keen sense that Travis and Janie had arranged this afternoon, and I think we both knew that we were safe with one another. I had never so much as kissed a girl, and I got the sense that Talia's experience with boys was comparable.

Talia didn't use her body to attract attention in the way that Janie did, and she came across like a girl who doubted her own beauty despite the fact that it was obvious. As for me, I was still a bit awkward and gangly and was just emerging from a swath of unattractive pimples that had adorned my face for a couple of years. I had all but given up on getting girls to look in my direction and figured I would have to wait until college to get a fresh start.

We walked down the trail for quite some time without saying a word when Talia grabbed my hand. She still didn't say anything, and we kept on walking. I wasn't sure what to do, but I felt her hand squeeze mine, and I squeezed hers with the same pressure. She bent her chin forward and laughed and I could see her smile. I was proving myself a willing, if unassuming, participant. It wasn't dark yet, but the sun was beginning to go down, and the trees around us had a golden tinge as evening moved in. There was nobody around, and we felt like we had the woods all to ourselves. Talia leaned her shoulder into mine, drawing her head close, and whispered, "Kyle, do you want to kiss me?

Of course, I did, but I couldn't find the words, and so I just stammered, "Yes" as Talia giggled sweetly. She pulled my hand gently and led me off the trail where she stood with her back to a big tree, shielding us from the view of the path even though nobody was on it. I leaned toward her slowly, craning my neck, and our noses bumped before I moved to the side and searched for her mouth with mine. Her lips sought mine out, and we fumbled around sweetly against the tree, practicing with one another tenderly, almost lovingly, in an attempt to understand what it meant to kiss and be kissed. We made a few awkward noises of delight, but only because we thought we were supposed to.

Then Talia placed her hands on my chest, and I stepped back and said, "Is everything alright?" when she said, "Would you like to touch me? I can tell you aren't like other boys, and I'd like it if you touched me."

Talia removed the tie from her ponytail and shook out her hair. Then she unbuttoned her blouse slowly, with the falling sun fixed upon her soft, white skin. I stood motionless, out of both respect and fear. Talia grabbed my hand again, this time placing it on her body's exposed flesh. She let me explore her torso with my hands and she helped guide them across her skin. I kissed her more convincingly than I had the first time, and she pulled my body tightly against hers so I could feel the warm sweat from her naked torso. After a few minutes, she whispered, almost apologetically, "It's starting to get late, Kyle. We should probably go back."

"Yes, of course. You're right," I said, stepping back while she began to button her blouse back up. She didn't seem shy anymore, and she even seemed to smile, taking her sweet time, so that I could enjoy watching her fasten each button until her white skin was no longer visible.

I wasn't much of a talker, but I did manage to say, "You are very beautiful," which seemed like a good choice based on her reaction.

We walked quicker on the way back in an attempt to make it to the swimming hole before it got dark. When we got there, Travis and Janie were sitting on a blanket. They were all dried off and their clothes were on. "You made it," said Travis. "We need to drive back around to the campground now on the other side of the lake."

I hopped in the truck with Travis, and Talia went with Janie as we headed back to pitch our tents, start a fire, and roast hot dogs. Travis got the wood positioned, and the fire was roaring in no time. He grabbed the beers from his truck, and we sat around the fire, eating and laughing and drinking beer, as the sun set and visions of the past few hours swirled through my head. For the first time in my life, I almost felt like a man, a real man.

It didn't take many beers for me to pass out, and I awoke, with Talia's head resting on my chest, to the sound of a woman's cries for help. There was another tent not far from ours, and the cries seemed to be coming from that direction. "Stay here," said Travis.

Travis leaped up wearing only his jeans, tossed me the keys to his truck (I'm not sure why), and stepped into his boots without a shirt. He ran over to the other tent, unzipped it, and we heard a voice say, "Get the fuck outta here, kid. This is none of your fucking business." The man turned his back to Travis, and Travis was able to get a clear view of the bruises on the woman's face, the marks all around her neck, and the fear in her eyes. It was at that moment that we saw what we somehow already knew Travis was capable of.

By way of shadows produced by the flashlight in the tent, we could see Travis reach in with both hands, grab the man from behind, and hurl him out of the tent and onto the dirt of the campground, while sounds escaped from the man's body that were somewhere between a groan and a growl. Travis then jumped on top of him. The man was strong in his own right, but Travis began punching him in the face with both hands, over and over and over. The man was fighting back, but it seemed like he was merely gasping for air, like someone drowning in the ocean.

He was no match for Travis, and we sat there and watched transfixed as Travis unleashed his fists one after the other, colliding his knuckles with the man's face amidst the screams and cries, until they stopped, and the man stopped. In many ways, it had seemed like the world itself had stopped, or at least for those few unmerciful minutes when Travis let his fury rain down on the man until he had extinguished his life. Travis was never going to stop. He couldn't stop, and his rage seemed the product of pure instinct that concluded with one man dead and another destined to be defined by this event.

Travis got off the man's body, made sure the woman was alright, and then covered him up with the blanket he and Janie had been sitting on at the water hole. The woman put her clothes on, and Travis told her to stay with us until he got back. He drove the man's car, and when he returned, he was sitting in the back seat of a police car, looking every bit as calm as the first time I had seen him. The policeman got out of the car and walked over to us to help determine what happened. He said Travis had driven to the police station and turned himself in. We gave our accounts of the story, how we just sat there, paralyzed, as Travis came to the aid of this woman and then beat the man savagely, unrelentingly, to a pulp.

The policeman thanked us and walked back to the car with Travis sitting in the back seat. Another policeman had arrived, and he spoke to the woman. She then got into his car, and they drove off, presumably to the police station or maybe the hospital. The man's inert body was loaded into an ambulance, which also drove off, though without any sirens or lights.

Janie stood up and said, "Talia, let's go." Talia hesitated, but she stood up and followed her cousin. I didn't know if I should call out to her, but she managed to look back at me. She was looking at me through the same eyes that had encouraged me to watch her get dressed, a look that said we were both somehow older, more experienced, than when the day began. It wasn't a look of longing or greed but rather one of both appreciation and satisfaction—despite having watched a man die.

I was alone next to the fire, which was merely smoldering now, but I could see Travis in the back of the police car. Although I had grown closer to becoming a man that afternoon, I would never be a man like him. I could never be a man like him. He had something inside him that came from a place I'd never know. It was something more primal, more unapologetically human. I think Travis knew that. I think he had always known that.

As the police car pulled out of the lot, Travis turned his head to look at me, wholly unaffected, just like he had been the first day I saw him at school. He still possessed the composure I had witnessed earlier that afternoon when he leaned over and kissed Janie, and the icy calm in his eyes illustrated none of the fear that might be associated with a young man who was headed to jail. He just stared at me with that look that said everything would be OK.

It was then I remembered I still had the keys, the keys to Travis's Chevy pickup. I walked over to the truck, opened the door, and slid into the driver's seat. I sat up straight behind the wheel and stared out the window past the flashing lights of the police car and into the night sky. I had kissed Talia, and I had watched a man die. I took one look in the rearview mirror, turned the engine over, and eased her onto the gravel road.

FISH THAT LEAP

In the mornings, the river was calm and smooth. It flowed steadily and without bias until it emptied into the sea. The air was cool before the sun rose and showered the dark waters with light that warmed my back but had little effect on the temperature of the river itself.

I walked to the edge, where the path sloped down and led gently into the water. I set my kayak in the cool water and climbed in carefully, making an effort not to upend the unstable bottom. It was a balancing act that was never as easy as I thought it should be. I'd been doing this for a long time, but the river still had the ability to surprise and catch me off guard. I didn't take anything for granted.

Seated, I stretched my legs forward and rested them at a comfortable angle. I grabbed the paddle with my right hand and then used the end of it to shove the kayak off the shoreline and toward the deeper waters. The moment I detached from the edge of the shore, there was a new feeling of freedom. It was the kind of freedom that a man can only feel untethered, floating alone, selfishly, in a river, distanced from all of the responsibilities that keep him grounded.

I paddled upstream first. This reminded me that even out here, in the open air, moving across the water, it takes effort, that real work was the only way if I was going to make it up the river. But I had the energy at the beginning of the day, and I took the adrenaline that had been building to launch me through the steady current. The body of the kayak was narrow and sleek, and it cut through the current easily.

I used to take a rowboat out so that I could fish ... and drink. Perhaps I really took it out so I could drink and do a little fishing. Drinking and fishing went well together, as Hemingway and Carver could attest. Cold beer. A warm day. The serene, peaceful waters. Casting. Over and over, just enough to make the world slide away, or give it a gentle shove toward the depths of blue water.

It wasn't long before the drinking came home with me. I returned loosened up and loose-lipped. Men who return home to their wives loose-lipped are bound to get into trouble. Men should always reveal what they feel, but they must do so with the filter of sensitivity, empathy, and understanding. Without those key elements, the validity of any sentiments is guaranteed to be met with scorn, or even worse … hostility.

And that's how I lost her. I lost her on the river, when the day came flowing so effortlessly with the reeds stacked all along the shore. The tall grass led the way, as the river snaked marvelously back and forth, each corner providing a new offering, a vantage point previously unconsidered.

Every now and again, I passed under a bridge. On a warm day, a bridge can provide just enough shade to make a difference, to make all the difference, if even only for a few seconds. Sometimes, a few seconds are just enough, to let the coolness wash over you, into you, before you emerge once again in the full, hot sun.

If land was a war chest of memories, then being on the water allowed those memories to flow more gently, even the painful ones. The sadness of loss seemed more palatable in a boat, easing along, rendering the sharpness of the pain almost unavailable while immersed in the fluidity of life.

On land, things were different. The demons chased me. They chased me like that man with no face who stalked my dreams as a child, moving methodically, relentlessly, until there was nowhere else to turn, until my luck had run out. And I knew my luck was destined to run out the longer I kept my feet upon the earth, the solid earth, with the overwhelming feeling of gravity. The earth was supposed to be stabilizing, but I never felt that way, not since I watched the ground open up to receive the bodies of my parents. The tranquility the river brought was something very different.

After all, when the paddle entered the water, it slid in so easily, so smoothly. It was nothing like the earth, where the labor of a shovel was required to pierce the soil and upend it. Water was just the opposite, both ready to carry you and receive you, propel you and calm you, envelope you and send you on your way, with the knowingness of solitude rather than the fear of it.

Near the middle of the day, I spotted a nice piece of shore and headed toward it. When I felt the bottom of the riverbed grab hold of my kayak, I used the paddle to maintain my balance, and I stepped out of the right side into the water up to my shins with my toes submerged in the slimy undercarriage of the river. I had packed a sandwich, and I sat on the shore and took it out and ate it and felt good.

Once I was done eating, I drank a bottle of water and then splashed the water of the river against my face and over the top of my head. I let my hands travel from my cheeks and eyes over the top of my head and down the back of my neck. It felt good in the hot sun, and I liked the smell of the river water on my face and skin. It made me feel like more of a man, with the smell of the river on the outside of my skin, and my body singing from the inside.

The afternoon seemed to be getting on, but it was still beautiful out, even more so as the sun began to fall. This would have been the time to drink beer in my rowboat, but I didn't drink beer anymore. And I didn't have a rowboat. Feeling the sun shining ever so slightly, I decided to climb back into my kayak and head down the river, gliding effortlessly, with the current behind me, and the momentum of the day's beauty steering me toward home.

It was then that I saw a fish leap out of the water, leap straight up into the air and then dive back down into the river. It caught me off guard, just as it did the first time I saw one surge out of the river all those years ago. I am not embarrassed to say it took my breath away then as it did now. The day I lost her, I had returned after drinking and fishing and seeing the fish emerge from the river for the first time. I wasn't used to being surprised on the river, to have the pace of my heart quicken, to have the capillaries rush forward with uncommon excitement.

The flight of the fish wasn't elegant like the flight of a dolphin, who bares its spine gloriously to the sky before rhythmically dipping back into the water. No. This was different. The fish popped out of the water with vigor, as if they themselves were surprised to discover the suffocating air, with the sun shining up above and the water's clear comfort below. They reentered the water hurriedly, with a sense of relief, as if merely having needed to check on the world above just to know it was there. I always admired the way they dove down with such certainty, such utter confidence that can only come from knowing where you belong.

Now I could see the point where I let my kayak into the water that morning. Much as I tried, there was no prolonging my arrival onshore. At this point, it was inevitable, and I moved like any man moves toward his destiny and away from it all at the same moment. All those years ago, I had walked in the front door of our house late at night to find her there waiting.

The children were already asleep, and I stood in our kitchen and told my wife about the fish who leaped out of the water for a moment only to realize the ramifications of this mistake and head back below the surface as quickly as possible. The great gravitational pull, as if the whole force of the earth's axis was in play, and everything was riding on it.

My wife just sat there and listened. She sat there and listened in the kitchen where we had fed our children for years, below the recessed lights that had cost a fortune when we remodeled our house, with her arms crossed in front of the island with a slab of granite on top. She had a glass of wine in her hand, and she cut a demure figure in the kitchen, even more refined and elegant than I remembered.

"You belong here," I remarked admiringly, although I could feel the condescension coming from her expression. It was resentment. Resentment for the unconcealed joy I had expressed at seeing the fish leap out of the water.

I was a good man, maybe even a great one, but I knew I would never be considered an easy one. Certainly not on land, where I still battled demons, where the faceless man still chased me in the night even when the sun was out. I had run down every corridor only to emerge gasping for breath, feeling the fleeting noose of life, like a fish out of water. Time and time again, she had come to my aid. She had listened, and she had been there by my side when the faceless man had me trapped in a corner, but she wasn't coming to the rescue this time. She just listened to me tell the story of the fish, and I knew then that the river would have to carry me from here.

"Just say it," I said. "Say it. I know you've been waiting for this moment for a long time," I said almost taunting her. "I can hardly blame you."

She pulled the glass to her lips, took a sip, and then set it back down on the island. The words almost seemed to come from somewhere else. They didn't seem real, couldn't be real, even if I had expected them. Perhaps I just never thought they would come so easily, so effortlessly, that they would flow out of her mouth like breath, as fluid as the river, snaking back and forth, guided by a steady, gentle current heading inevitably from source to mouth, the only possible destination.

THE ANNIVERSARY

The last time he took Mom out, she wasn't even there. I mean, she was there physically, but that was about it.

Her medication was strong, but she was weak and frail. We got her dressed at home, helping her get her arms in the sleeves of her shirt and fasten the buttons down the front. Dad and I had her sit on the bed to help her with her pants, and she just sat there. The bedsores were the worst they had been, but she didn't complain. She never complained.

We asked her if she would prefer to stay in. "No," she said. "It's our anniversary."

"We can celebrate here," my father suggested. "Have a nice meal brought in."

"No," she reiterated. "It's our anniversary. We'll go out."

I remember looking at her when she was sitting on the bed. I wasn't sure if she was still there, if she was still in the room. For just a moment, a blank look had come across her face. It wasn't a look of pain or despair. There was no trace of pain. None at all. It was as if she was no longer my mother, as if her spirit, her essence, had already departed.

A moment later, the look faded. She asked for her shoes, the black ones with the high heels.

"Are you sure you want to wear those shoes?" I asked.

"Of course," she said. "They're beautiful."

My father knew better than to question her. "I'll get them," he said. "I know you love those shoes."

We worked to fit them over her feet. They had some bruising, and they were more fragile than I remembered. Although she didn't seem comfortable when we fastened the straps, she didn't complain or even wince. She just said, "Thank you. That's fine." She said it plain, in the most dignified manner.

Her hair was more difficult. It had vanished as a result of the chemotherapy. She had a generous selection of wigs that she kept in front of her mirror. The women at the store had done their best to match her natural hair color or, rather, the color she had dyed her hair for years. It wasn't perfect, but it wasn't all that bad either. The styles were more difficult, and it wasn't easy to select one that didn't look like a helmet. Still, she didn't hesitate. She hardly ever hesitated, and she picked one, placed it atop her head, and arranged it the best way she could. No fuss. Afterward, she did her makeup, and she tried to add color to her face now that her skin had become yellowish and gray. It was as if the life was leaking out of her body, and the lack of color in her face only accentuated this reality.

Then, in a moment, almost as if she had accepted the reality that this was as presentable as she was going to be able to make herself look, she said, "Let's go."

Of course, she wasn't able to move quickly. Her strength had deteriorated, and the process of getting ready had also taken a toll. My father and I helped her to her feet, and then my father went to pull the car out of the garage. My mother hooked her arm inside mine, and I walked her carefully to the passenger's side door. It was beginning to drizzle, and we walked slowly. My mother didn't say a word, but I could feel her leaning toward me, partly in apology, partly in appreciation. It was a strange feeling. Mothers aren't supposed to apologize to their sons, even silently. It's supposed to be the other way around.

I opened the door with her arm still hooked inside mine and helped her shuffle close to the side of the car. Supporting her back, I eased her into the seat carefully with my father looking on. Once my mom was sitting, I lifted her legs over the side of the car and placed them underneath the glove box with the warm vents blowing on her cold, exposed feet in the high heels. She feigned a smile, and I closed the door.

I watched her as my dad backed the car to the edge of the driveway. The look on her face told me she had gone somewhere else again. It had the same blankness I noticed in the bedroom, far away, perhaps to a place where everything just disappeared. My father gently put his foot on the brakes before backing into the street. He wasn't the kind of man to give a compliment or even an acknowledgment, but he winked at me before he pulled out into the street. He winked, and he nodded his head. It was as close to an endorsement as I had ever received.

The rain was falling now. The wipers were sliding back and forth across the windshield. My parents were going out to dinner. They were going out to dinner, just as they had so many times before. I watched the taillights disappear in the distance with the rain falling softly and the night sky moving in. My parents, going out to dinner for the last time.

THE MILKMAN

There were things he couldn't remember, but he remembered when he used to deliver milk. When he used to deliver milk in glass bottles, cold glass bottles, to houses throughout the neighborhood.

This was a long time ago, in the days when everyone had a milkman, much like a garbageman, who arrived at your house each week in a truck carrying milk. Many homes were even constructed specifically with the milkman in mind, with refrigerated storage for milk bottles embedded right in the walls.

He had developed his love of milk from a young age. In summers as a boy, he worked on his grandpa's farm, doing odd jobs in the barn and milking the cows. This allowed him to learn the importance of milk, see its origins, and understand just how many steps were involved in the process of getting milk to all the people who consumed it. There was nothing easy about it but, even as a boy, he liked the feeling that he was doing something that mattered, that his efforts weren't for naught, and that the world needed people like him.

In the '60s, the country was at a crossroads with the war in Vietnam, civil rights, and a cultural sea change. But people still needed milk, and it was often the milkman who brought it to them. He remembered this time well, liked this time in history, when the simple things were still simple. His life was simple, his work unchanged by outside revolutions. And he delivered the milk on time, each day, each week, throughout the year with perfect syncopation.

This allowed him to turn his eyes away from other societal complexities. He could focus solely on his own craft, the elements of his work where he could strive for perfection in such a wholly imperfect world. Being a milkman provided a sense of order, from the delivery to the manner in which he lined up the bottles in each home. There was nothing chaotic about it, and order was both possible and comforting. It made sense to him.

Everything was different now. He never wanted to stop working, couldn't stop working, and he continued to work as a milkman of sorts. Today that meant working in a large supermarket, in the dairy section.

His job had changed, and he missed the days when he brought milk to the customers. But he had adapted too, and he knew every brand they carried, where it was produced, if it was organic, the difference in the various fat contents, and so on. People deferred to him as a sort of expert in his field, and customers still sought the old man out for his knowledge. Not many employees went back to the days of milkmen, but he did, and he was valued for it.

In those days, he usually delivered the milk in the morning, after husbands had gone to work and kids had departed for school. Oftentimes, this simply meant leaving the milk in a milk chute, but other times women invited him inside to place the bottles of milk in the refrigerators. Although this could have been awkward, he was always professional, and he made the deliveries swiftly and efficiently.

He wore a pair of white trousers and a white shirt. They all did, but he dressed the stereotype to a tee, complete with black shoes and a bow tie and a cap. The shirt was a button-down, but it had short sleeves, which helped reveal his strong physique. He had strong arms and a strong chin and, even in a milkman's uniform, there was something about him that was overwhelmingly manly.

For a man who knew just about everything about milk, he was relatively naive about the world. He was what they would have called "square" in those days. He'd been a good student. He'd served his country in the Navy. He didn't drink alcohol, and he was never known to be found carousing around town with women. He was smart, and he should have seen it coming, but it's also not terribly surprising he didn't.

Mrs. Stansfield was a new bride, slightly older than he was, and the neighborhood had been surprised when she separated from her husband. He was a prominent lawyer in town, and they hadn't even been married a year. But it wasn't long before the rumors began to circulate. Some said he beat her. Others said she had been unfaithful. And a few people insisted that he preferred men. There must have been a dozen stories floating around, and the validity of each was up for debate in the court of public opinion.

What was not up for debate was Mrs. Stansfield's beauty. She had chiseled cheekbones, intoxicating green eyes, and a smile that ran from ear to ear and could level a man if she chose to flash it. She had a tall, slender figure and, by the looks of it, came from money, real money, the kind with gold cigarette cases and designer dresses for every day of the week. Her hair was long and straight, naturally strawberry blonde and might as well have been metallic the way it radiated in the light.

He had seen attractive women before, but she was different. She wasn't merely attractive. She had class, and she moved with the kind of elegance that reminded him of what it meant to be a man and made him forget everything else all at once. She had the kind of beauty that could erase a man's memory just with the sound of her breathy voice. She was, in a word, spectacular.

This wasn't news to anyone, and it caused nearly everyone to keep a safe distance. Mrs. Stansfield's beauty was overwhelming and intimidating, and she was well aware of this. She reluctantly accepted the isolation that came with this type of beauty, and she simply went about her days, completing tasks and now living alone. She had to be well aware of the power she possessed, and, to her credit, she chose not to wield it for her own personal gain.

He had been delivering milk to Mrs. Stansfield for quite some time. He had seen her husband a few times before their separation, since he left for work later on some days, when he was going straight from home to visit a client. Although he always said hello to Mr. Stansfield and tipped his cap, he couldn't remember Mr. Stansfield ever responding.

Mrs. Stansfield was one of those customers who always preferred he place the milk in the refrigerator, which made things easier for her. He was more than happy to oblige, and he always pulled the milk truck up the driveway along the side of the house, which was close to the entrance by the kitchen. There were a couple of steps up to the door, and then he would enter, turn left and kneel down to place the milk bottles in the refrigerated cupboards that were embedded in the wall. He barely looked up, trying to keep his focus on the task at hand, but he could see that the house was well-appointed.

He could also see Mrs. Stansfield, who often leaned against the wall, holding a cup of coffee almost regally, while he placed the milk bottles in a neat, lined manner. He didn't get the feeling that she was watching him in order to make sure he did his job correctly, but she certainly watched him, if somewhat indifferently.

Each week, he simply walked in the door, said a pleasant hello that she returned, dropped off the milk bottles, and was on his way. She never offered him so much as a glass of water, and he made sure never to overstay his welcome. It was like this during the months when Mr. Stansfield was living there and after he had moved out. Nothing changed, and he made sure the delivery was on time.

On the week following Labor Day, he arrived at Mrs. Stansfield's house on Tuesday. He pulled down the driveway and entered the back door just as he usually did. It was a hot morning, and he was perspiring, so he enjoyed the feeling of the coolness of the refrigerator when he opened the door to place the bottles inside.

"I was expecting you yesterday," she said, engaging in conversation with him that was very much out of character.

"Normally, I would have come on Monday, ma'am," he replied. "But yesterday was a holiday."

"Even so," she quipped. "I didn't know you took holidays off."

"Yes, we do, ma'am," he answered flatly. "I am sorry you had to wait an extra day."

"It's fine," she said, standing against the wall sipping her coffee and smiling generously.

It was unlike her to smile and make easy conversation. It was unlike her, and it made him nervous. He wasn't used to making conversation with her, and part of him wished they could return to their regular, sterile interaction.

But he could see that she seemed to be enjoying herself. Certainly, she was enjoying herself more than he was, and this was not lost on him. Although she clearly knew her immense beauty made men uncomfortable, this time she seemed to be genuinely enjoying it—particularly since he remained the perfect gentleman as always.

It was then that she turned her back to him quite gracefully and let her summer dress fall to the floor around her feet. She stepped out of the dress wearing nothing but her low-heeled shoes and walked out of the kitchen as he fumbled to place the last bottle in the refrigerator.

She didn't have to tell him to follow her, but she did say to "bring a bottle of milk" as she turned right and walked up the stairs.

He was, in every way, a reasonable man, but this was a moment when reason was overpowered by his most primal human instincts, when his response was so natural that it could not be questioned or given a second thought. This was one of those moments, and he remembers calmly closing the refrigerator door and walking up the stairs with the bottle of milk in one hand.

Mrs. Stansfield could hear when he got to the top of the stairs, and she said, "Last door on the right," without a hint of nervousness or acceleration in her tone. She appeared completely in control, more than ever in fact, and he now felt like little more than a subject, willing to do whatever he was told.

When he walked into the room, she had already removed the sheets and blankets. There was nothing but a white top sheet over the mattress, and he found her sitting on the bed with her back to the headboard and her legs crossed in the manner they might be if she were sitting in a chair, with one knee folded over the other. She then placed both hands on the end of her top knee, and she was still wearing her low-heeled shoes in the bed.

"You can set the bottle of milk on the nightstand," she let him know.

"Yes, ma'am," he said, still trying to act professional, even though they were now on much more intimate terms it seemed.

"And won't you please help a lady with her shoes?" she asked politely. "I am a lady, after all."

He walked to the edge of the bed, losing the battle with his quickening heart rate, and slid her left shoe off her foot. He made sure to do so with great care, slipping her heel out delicately and taking the opportunity to feel the soft skin on her feet, which had obviously been well cared for.

He took the time to treat each foot equally, and he could tell she appreciated his ability to control himself and play along well. It wasn't so different from the manner in which he delivered the milk each week, although there was nothing routine about the moment he found himself in.

"I'm thirsty," she said, now sitting completely naked in the bed. He had never seen a woman so completely comfortable with her naked body, void of any insecurities, and utterly satisfied with her womanly perfection.

He walked to the bedside table and handed her the cold bottle of milk and then sat beside her torso. She smiled as she drank the milk from the bottle.

"Your turn," she said with a smile. "Shirt first and take your time."

The milkman took his time, and he found himself to be surprisingly calm as he took off his clothes. He wasn't prepared for this, to feel so calm in her presence. But she had made him feel this way. For all her external beauty, it was her beauty inside that seemed to flow from her naked body while she sat on the bed, drank milk, and smiled like an innocent girl.

She looked so happy, genuinely happy, and she threw her head back, laughing, while the milk spilled down her chin. She poured some more milk down her perfectly formed breasts, uncrossed her legs, and laughed as she welcomed his body into hers.

After their bodies had joined and come apart, they spent a long time lying in the bed together, saying nothing. She had a cigarette from her gold case and asked him if he would like one, which he politely declined, since he didn't smoke.

He didn't particularly like smoking either, but he had to admit that Mrs. Stansfield could even make smoking a cigarette look elegant and attractive. She then exhaled with her eyes closed, leaned her head against his shoulder, and began to cry.

The tears poured down her face as if they had been released from a thousand years of captivity. They burst forth, and they ran down her cheeks, as soft, painful cries leaked out of her perfect body. The milkman reached his left hand across her face and gently wiped the tears from her cheeks that still sat prominently below her swollen eyes. They still hadn't said a word since she had asked him to undress. She needed him not to say a word and, somehow, he knew not to.

She cried some more and held on to him and said nothing, as uninhibited with her tears as she had been with her body. Each time he wiped them away without saying a word. They stayed together until the afternoon when it was time for each of them to part ways. He got dressed while she remained in the bed, now with the covers pulled over her to keep warm in his absence.

He kissed her on the cheek and spoke to her lovingly.

"Mrs. Stansfield, I am a man of limited experience. I am not worldly, and I deliver milk," he said. "But I am sure of one thing. There is no woman like you anywhere on earth. Of this, and only this, am I certain."

She looked at him coolly now, much like she did each week when he delivered the milk. Her tears were pushed back now, pushed back down, and her green eyes were alive again. Her confidence had returned.

"This can't possibly come as a surprise to you," she said, tossing her head back with complete seriousness. "Of course, there isn't a woman alive who compares to me."

He hoped she believed it. He sincerely hoped she did. It was true, after all, and he smiled, tipped his cap, exited the bedroom, and let himself out.

The next week he arrived at Mrs. Stansfield's home on Monday, at the same time he always did. There were no cars in the driveway, and a For Sale sign had been placed on the lawn. Even so, he parked his milk truck the way he always did and walked to the back door. He rang the bell, but it was clear nobody was home.

When he walked back around to the front to peer in a window, he saw that the house was empty. The lights were out, and the furniture had been removed. Mrs. Stansfield was gone.

Just as they had emerged regarding her marriage, rumors began to take flight. Some said her divorce had been finalized and she had left as planned. Others whispered she had run off with someone else. And one rumor even persisted that her husband's sterility was to blame.

The milkman was left with something else. Of course, he heard all the rumors, but he also held the secret of the day they had spent together, in one another's arms. Did that day play a role in her departure or was it already planned? And if it was all part of a plan, what role had he played? Did she use him for the comfort of a stranger's arms or something more serious? What if she was hoping, with a sterile husband, for him to give her a child? As if the memory of her beauty wasn't enough, these questions persisted in his mind almost to the point of madness. It was too much, far too much, for him to consider.

For a time, he looked for her. And he asked a few innocuous questions around town, but there was no information regarding her whereabouts. After a while, even the rumors stopped circulating, and there was little doubt that Mrs. Stansfield had vanished permanently.

This was all such a long time ago. Milking the cows on his grandpa's farm. Delivering milk bottles in a truck. And the unforgettable afternoon with Mrs. Stansfield. The afternoon that would stay with him, etched in time. Decades had come and gone, and a host of memories had merely slid away like silt on a river. But there are some things you never forget, even when time moves on in its merciless pursuit of days.

Was it the beginning of the end or the end of the beginning? It was hard to tell, and it depended on his perspective. He never married, and he had no children. But he kept working in the day and the night. Sometimes he drove past Mrs. Stansfield's house.

It hadn't changed much. Back at the supermarket, he always made sure the cartons and bottles were lined perfectly. Most of his younger colleagues never even knew his name. They just called him "The Milkman."

ALL THAT REMAINED

There was nothing Dr. Sampson did in his job that was more difficult. It didn't matter how prepared he was or if he accepted this was part of the job, that it came with the territory in his profession. These things didn't help, not really. Not in the moment. Not when it was only him who was left to deliver the news.

He wasn't a priest after all. He was a doctor, albeit one who had dedicated his life to treating patients with cancer. Of course, he had considered all of this many years before, when he chose medicine and selected this specialty. But he was young then. He was far enough from truly considering his own mortality to be beautifully naive about what he might be able to handle and where he could make the biggest difference.

Dr. Sampson had made a difference, a real difference in the lives of so many patients. And he was proud of this. But he had changed over time. Age slowly chips away at the unbridled optimism of youth. Now the victories seemed hollow, while he took the losses harder than ever. The joy he once felt upon seeing a patient cured was now replaced with relief. At the same time, the pragmatic acceptance of the possibility of death had now been replaced by a sense of personal failure and heartbreak. His unflappable nerves now appeared terribly human, and they began to destroy him.

That's when the drinking started. At first, it was just a quick stop at a bar on the way home. Even though he was alone, he didn't sit at the bar. If you sat at the bar, it always seemed like you were expected to talk—whether that was exchanging pleasantries with the bartender or the person next to you. And he didn't feel like talking. Not after he had just left the hospital. He didn't feel like talking at all, and he picked a small booth in the corner, where he could slump his back against the wood and take his Scotch neat ... and in silence. For a while, this calmed his nerves, at least a little, enough to appear something like a functioning human being when he returned home to his wife and kids.

At home, the expectations were different. His children were still small, and they ran to the door with great enthusiasm when he arrived. They tugged at his coat gleefully. No matter what had happened during the day, he had to, at the very least, meet their enthusiasm with something that resembled excitement. The drink helped take the edge off, and he tried to immerse himself in their worlds until they went to sleep each night.

Once they were in bed, the color would drain from his face. He appeared sallow and gaunt and broken. He would go to the fridge to see what food remained from the dinner he had missed. Then he rummaged over the cold shelves like a starving animal. He would heat up anything that was quick and easy and sit at the table with one small recessed light overhead.

There was something savage about the manner in which he ate his food. Many days he was forced to skip lunch, and between the empty stomach, the torment of the job, and the recent lubrication with Scotch, he tore into his meal like a man who hadn't eaten in weeks.

These behaviors were almost like a return to the most primal human instincts. He spoke little, and he possessed qualities resembling a caveman at these moments. When he was finished and he had time to reflect, he came to the conclusion that this was a response to the pragmatic, almost inhuman facade he had to put on at various times throughout the day. Of course, he tried to exhibit the best of humanity with his patients, but he also had to deliver sobering news with professionalism and poise. This required a level of detachment, and it also served as a necessity for his own self-preservation. He couldn't live and die with every result, even if his patients did. It was such a strange existence, and his behavior in front of a plate of food was the manifestation of a completely natural response to what he had been through during the course of the day.

There were even times when he found himself crying as he sat over a steak or a platter of chicken, tears streaming down his face as he fastened his fork to the meat and moved his knife back and forth. These wild flushes of emotion were prone to arrive at any time, once he had let his guard down and allowed himself to feel. He wouldn't be able to function like this during the day, but it felt healthy now, therapeutic even—if somewhat painful and embarrassing.

Most of all, he didn't like crying in front of his wife, at least not over his job. Although she usually ate with the kids, she liked to sit with him at the table while he ate his dinner, often with a glass of wine in her hand. She had made the food, after all, on the heels of her own workday, and she enjoyed watching him eat it with so much enthusiasm. It was a small thing but an important one.

Still, she knew he was far away. When the veneer came off, he felt far away, no matter how hard he tried not to. He loved his wife because he could be himself with her, but that meant taking his work home and carrying it around like a millstone. That's what it was, after all, if he was honest. But his wife didn't deserve his work to consume their personal life, to dominate his psyche to the point of obsession, and so he tried to balance this—unsuccessfully he felt. He was either an emotional pincushion or distant and cold.

He felt closest to her when they made love, not because he craved a solely physical relationship with his wife, but rather because this was a place where he could express his emotions without speaking. When their bodies were intertwined, he could allow everything inside him to come rushing forth—the pain and sadness and anger and love and devotion gathering momentum and transferring from his body into hers. After they were finished, he would wrap his arms around her warm skin and fall asleep with the full weight of his body, his soul, collapsed against the freckled skin of her back.

He never remembered his dreams, but he had frequent nightmares. He would wake up gasping for breath, to find the comfort of his wife's hand on his chest and the soothing sound of her voice. "You're OK," she would reiterate. "You just had a nightmare."

Some nights he stayed awake after these episodes. He would sit on the couch in the dark and just stare into the blackness of the windowpanes in the quiet. But most nights he was able to go back to sleep. She helped him feel as if everything would be OK, and they didn't talk about it in the morning, after they were both fully awake and the water of the shower had washed the nighttime sweat off their bodies.

Eventually, he started drinking earlier in the day. Never on a day he performed surgery but still quite often. An Irish coffee here. A swig of his flask there. Where a drink had once taken the edge off, now it increased his fragility, his volatility, sent his moods up and down, and it began to erode his relationships. He managed to keep this from his patients and colleagues, but everyone else in his life suffered.

After work, he started to return home later and later. One drink would turn into two and two to three. Always alone. That never changed, but he was plunging deeper into his own psyche. He stopped thinking about everyone else. His problems, his stress, were greater than other people's. How could they not be? They had to be. And if he stopped just short of feeling sorry for himself, he had fallen to the point where he could no longer think clearly. He could hardly believe there was a time when he was so brash, so self-assured and hopeful, that he had made a conscious choice to go out and work to obtain this life.

Looking back, the night Dr. Sampson wrapped his Mercedes around a telephone pole was a blessing. Despite the compound fracture in his right leg, a plethora of lacerations, and some internal bleeding, he was incredibly fortunate. He had been going too fast. Way too fast. He was under the influence of alcohol. And yet, he was alive. Nobody else had been hurt, and his brain was very much intact. Doctors said he would make a full recovery. He took a medical leave from the hospital, got sober, and paid his debt to society through a fine and hours of community service. Before the crash, he had been hurtling through each day toward imminent self-destruction. The truth was that the accident had saved his life.

When the smoke cleared and he had made a full recovery, his wife was gone. He had lost her months earlier, and she had taken the kids with her to her mother's. She hadn't wanted to serve him with the divorce papers while he was in the hospital. But when he returned home from the alcohol rehabilitation facility, they were waiting for him, laid out on the dining room table, complete with a pen, set aside for him to sign. He tried to plead with her to come back with the kids, but she told him that ship had sailed. It had sailed long before his accident, and everyone had known it but him. She was happy he had gotten sober. This gave her hope that he might become a positive influence in their children's lives, but she was done. She was utterly done, and there was no coming back.

He sat in the house that they had built together. He sat at the island in the kitchen she had remodeled so beautifully. His medical leave was almost over, and he contemplated the future, his future. He had figured he would transition out of his profession, maybe into an administrative role, but now he wasn't so sure. Who would he be doing it for? His wife and kids were gone. She had full custody, and she had relegated him (rightfully so) to a weekend dad—once or twice a month if he was lucky.

All that remained were his patients. His sick patients. His faithful patients. They had counted on him before and, those who were still fighting the disease, were counting on him still. His patients. His brave and scared patients. He felt this, was drawn to it. They were all he had left, and for the first time in years, he felt an unearthly calm come over him.

The next morning, Dr. Sampson woke up, dressed for work, and took a cup of coffee in the awkward loneliness of his kitchen. It was cold outside. He got behind the wheel of his car, pulled his leather gloves over his fingers, and turned on the heater. He drove to the hospital as he had done so many times before. He had lost nearly everything, but he was alive. He was remarkably alive and, more importantly, there were still people who counted on him to be at his best.

Mr. Reynolds was his first patient of the day. Dr. Sampson had gone over his paperwork beforehand and acquainted himself with the most recent test results. His own brush with death had changed him. He had felt the randomness of it all, the pure strokes of luck that determined why some people live and others die.

And he sat down with the professional, detached compassion he had once exhibited before the job had gotten the best of him.

"Mr. Reynolds," he said. "I'm sorry. I've got some bad news for you."

THE RIVERBOAT CASINO

I was pulling the metallic lever on the slot machine when she came by and asked if I wanted a drink. She was tall, perhaps just a few inches under six feet, with short brown hair that was styled attractively above her face with brown eyes and a warm, wide smile. She had an athletic body that was easily visible beneath the somewhat revealing cocktail dress she wore while she took orders and brought drinks.

When she stopped next to my chair, I was caught looking into her eyes and hesitated to say anything before realizing I was probably staring inappropriately. I looked down and smiled before looking up again, this time to order my drink.

"Gin and tonic, please," I asked.

"Got it," she said, before asking, "Lime?"

"Yes," I said. "What else would I have in it?"

"Well," she said flatly, "lately, it seems lots of people, men in particular, are asking for a lemon in their G and Ts, beers too."

"Not sure what kind of men want a lemon in their gin and tonics, let alone their beers," I replied. "Europeans?"

"All kinds," said the waitress. "My boyfriend for one."

She went out of her way to mention that she had a boyfriend, although her motivation was unclear. Was this to let me know she was in a relationship? Perhaps. At the same time, she seemed happy to let me know he was one of those I had subtly disparaged with my lemon comment. Either way, it caught me off guard, though I didn't show it.

I didn't say anything and just nodded. I was minding my own business, after all, and I certainly wasn't looking to cause any trouble. She seemed surprised I hadn't reacted more strongly.

"That doesn't bother you?" she asked. "That I have a boyfriend?"

"Why would it bother me?" I asked. "Seems perfectly fine and not unexpected. You're an attractive woman."

She blushed a bit. She was flirting with me in her own way, mostly to see how I would react it seemed, although the blushing seemed to come from someplace genuine.

I decided to follow up my comment to make things clear. "I only asked for a gin and tonic," I said. "You were the one who tried to make conversation."

"Well, excuse me for being friendly," she remarked, slightly offended. "Just a little Midwestern hospitality."

"That's fine," I said. "I like hospitality as much as the next guy. It's nice that you're friendly." I tipped my cap and added formally, "Ma'am," to make sure she knew I was respectful and that I got the message.

"You're not from around here, are you?" she asked.

"Where's here?" I asked, interested to get her definition of "here."

"Kansas," she said. "Kansas City to be more specific."

"No, I'm not," I replied. "If I was, do you think I'd be here, pulling slots on a riverboat casino on a Tuesday night?"

"Maybe," she said. "Not all that much to do here. Plenty of locals come to this place too. You'd be surprised."

I wasn't all that surprised to be honest, but I didn't let on. It seemed easier just to allow her to make her point. It also let the conversation come to a natural pause, where she likely realized I was still without a drink. "Let me grab you that drink," she said, a little more reserved this time.

She brought me the gin and tonic quicker than expected. It was stronger than I usually found at casinos, where they often watered down the drinks. I asked her if she wouldn't mind extending my compliments to the bartender, and I gave her a good tip as well. The drink was also fashioned with a cut lime, and the highball glass was nice as well. I had to admit it exceeded my expectations for a drink at a riverboat casino.

"Not bad, huh?" she said.

"It's perfect."

"Sure you wouldn't like it better with a lemon?" she smirked.

"I'm sure," I said. "Very sure."

I laughed and put more money in the slot machine. "You want to take a spin?" I asked her. "Lady Luck and all that."

"Thanks, but I am not allowed," she said. "The boss frowns on it, and they have cameras everywhere."

"Sure. I understand."

"Another time, maybe?" she inquired almost wistfully.

"Absolutely," I said. "Another time."

"Let me make another run of drinks and then I'll come back," she said. "You're fun to talk to. Different than other guys I've met."

She turned and pirouetted away with an empty tray before I could even respond but just long enough to catch another glimpse of her walking on air it seemed, across the gaudy casino carpet. It might have been the alcohol talking, but I found myself intrigued just enough to want to know more about her, despite her acknowledged attachments.

When she got back, she brought me another gin and tonic, even though I hadn't ordered one yet. I had just finished the first one and had to admit her timing and her instincts were good.

"Thank you," I said and nodded. "Appreciate it."

"Sure," she said, now playing coy. "Figured you might want another."

"So, where's your boyfriend tonight?" I asked, figuring I had nothing to lose and not caring all that much about him since I wasn't sure she did either.

"He's out with his friends," she responded. "Or at least that's what he tells me."

"What he tells you?" I asked. "You mean you don't trust him?"

"No, I don't," she said. "He's a liar. He's always been a liar. And I caught him with another woman once when he said he was going to his parents' house for dinner. Just happened to go by his place, since I forgot the shoes I needed for work. So no, I don't trust him."

I wasn't sure why she felt like she could talk to me. Maybe it was because I didn't act overly interested. I wasn't sure, but she wanted to talk, seemed she needed to talk, and it was clear she felt like she could say just about anything to me. I suppose, above all, I was a stranger and someone she was unlikely to see again. That, in itself, offered safety.

"So why do you stay with a guy like that?" I responded, asking the most obvious question ever.

"I don't know," she said, now looking deflated. "Loneliness, maybe."

"There are other guys," I said, "who will treat you better."

"Really?" she asked. "Are there? Guys who would treat me better. Because this has been my experience with guys."

"The wrong guys," I interjected.

"All guys," she said, "if I am being perfectly honest."

In the time that we had begun talking about her boyfriend, I'd literally seen the color drain from her face. There was no longer a trace of the vivacious woman who had participated in the friendly banter earlier that night. The polished veneer she put forth had worn thin, and I could now see her vulnerability and doubt. In its own way, it was as attractive as the swagger she had exhibited when we first interacted. It was a bit more human, more natural, almost lacking in confidence, humble, despite her obvious assets.

"You're beautiful," I said boldly. "Very beautiful. You can be playful and witty and charming and you're smart. I've seen all that in just a few minutes. You shouldn't forget that."

She blushed again, though this time differently. I could tell she was flattered, even if she didn't quite believe me.

"You really think so?" she said. "Or are you just sweet-talking me like all the others?"

"I am sure of it," I said. "And I barely know you. But I know enough to realize you shouldn't settle. Nobody should settle, really, but not everyone has your options."

"My options?"

"Yes," I said. "Unlimited options. Brains. Beauty. Humor. Wit. I am pretty sure that you can be choosy when it comes to men."

"I haven't been," she said. "Or I haven't been attracted to the right men ... or chosen them at least."

"Why not?" I asked.

"Sometimes," she hesitated, almost as if she wondered if she should reveal it, "sometimes, I just, I just worry whether anyone will ever love me. Just love me, that's it. That's all I am really asking for, looking for. Someone to love and someone who will love me."

I couldn't follow that up. Not appropriately, or genuinely, anyway. I didn't know why she felt unloved, but I couldn't very well tell her I loved her either. We had only just met, but I liked her. I liked her a lot. She wasn't just beautiful. She was luminous and transparent. And with each layer she pulled back, my attraction to her seemed to grow. If she had first caught my attention with her long, strong body and her warm, dark eyes, she now kept it with something of an open, broken heart—clichéd as that may sound. But I knew that I liked her, and I told her so.

"I like you," I said. "From the moment I saw your warm, brown eyes, I knew I liked you."

"But you don't love me."

"Love you? I don't know you well enough to love you," I said. "We've only just met."

"I don't know why," she went on, "but I believe you. The words don't sound like a line or like hot air."

"I am glad," I said. "It's the truth."

"The truth," she ruminated. "That's a funny word. What is the truth?"

"Reality?" I offered up. "Something that is real, authentic."

"Everyone has a different take on reality," she said. "For example, did you come in here tonight looking to meet someone?"

"No," I said flatly.

"Hoping?" she followed up.

"Well …," I said, smiling, "I am always hoping. But it's just not that easy."

She laughed. It seemed like she had gotten some of her confidence back. Perhaps it was due to my compliments or the feeling that I was showing interest in her or maybe it was just due to a protective mechanism that was ingrained. But she appeared somehow more relaxed now and less vulnerable than she had been a few moments before. Although I didn't know her well, I knew that she couldn't be pinned down, confined, to being just one thing. She was a chameleon. Her personality spanned a wide spectrum. Perhaps that's true of everyone to some extent, but she had revealed that vast expanse of hers in only a few short minutes, and it was terribly endearing, intoxicating really.

"I'd like to see you," I said. "Would you have dinner with me this week?"

"What's next?" she snapped. "You going to tell me to quit my job? Promise to take me away from all this?"

"I was just thinking of a nice meal. Engaging conversation. A chance to get to know one another. A first date, I think they call it."

"Is that all?"

"Yes, that's all," I said. "Why would I want to take you away from all this?" I added.

"Ha. Very funny," she deadpanned. "Why? Because everyone else does."

"Well, I am not everyone else," I stated emphatically.

"Clearly," she said, happy, if slightly annoyed.

"My whole life people have been trying to change me," she said. "And every guy I meet wants to 'take me away' from this job."

"Perhaps to keep you from meeting guys like me," I suggested.

"Perhaps. But I think it's less about meeting guys like you than it is about controlling me, them deciding what's best for me."

"You can do that for yourself," I added confidently.

"They don't think so," she said.

"The nice thing is they don't get to choose," I said. "You do."

"True. But it's exhausting to always feel like the people around you wish you were different and want to change you. Think they can change you."

"Nobody can change anyone," I said.

"Do you really believe that?"

"Yes, I do," I said. "At least not at their core. I don't think that our DNA can be altered by another person. It's just woven too tight, for better or worse."

"So, do you believe people are incapable of growth?" she asked, probing deeper. "Are we incapable of real evolution?"

She had my attention. She had my full attention. If I am honest, I hadn't pegged this riverboat casino for a place to engage in an intellectual debate about the human capacity for change, but here I was digging in.

"I think we can grow," I responded. "Absolutely. And I think we have the power to change our behavior, to 'evolve' as you say regarding the manner in which we might go about things. Behavior we can change, but personality … that's something else. I believe we are who we are in this regard at the moment of our wiring."

"So, you don't want to change my wiring?" she asked.

"I can't," I responded, if only to support my hypothesis. "But I wouldn't still be talking to you if I did."

"Good answer," she smiled again, even warmer this time.

"So, dinner?" I repeated. "Any more thoughts about that?"

"I get off work at two," she replied. "A girl's got to eat."

"Well, how about another night this week? I was thinking of a nice place … that isn't open at two in the morning."

"Are you trying to change me already?"

"I am not, honest—," I said, but she cut me off.

"Relax, I like to eat when I get off work," she said. "I am going to grab a bite at two o'clock with or without you."

She didn't sound desperate now. She sounded confident and brash. But I had seen too much. I knew this was only one aspect of her personality. With or without me. Damn. What a woman she was. What an incredible woman she was. I knew it. Somehow, I knew it, deep down in my core, in my wiring, the moment she asked about the lemon in my gin and tonic, the moment she flashed those browns that cut down deep and sliced the conversation like a surgeon.

"In that case, I choose 'with' as in 'with' me," I said. "You can grab a bite with me. My treat."

"That sounds lovely," she said, seemingly satisfied.

Inside the casino, it was difficult to tell what time it was. The lights flashing, the machines dinging from all directions. No visible windows. In just a few moments, I lost all sense of the time. And in one evening, it seemed as if my past and future had suddenly blurred. I was moving slow and fast all at the same time. And I couldn't stop it.

One minute, I tried to get my mind to slow down and then next I was unable to get it to keep up. It was as if the earth's axis had turned. I may not have fundamentally changed, but I felt a shift.

"Perfect," I said. Although I was new in town, I had seen a classic-looking twenty-four-hour diner on the way in, and it was just a few blocks away. She seemed to read my mind.

"Great," she said. "I know just the place."

EVEN AFTER ALL THESE YEARS

It was impossible to forget that night, even after all of these years. It was raining. It was raining hard, a hard, Southern rain where the sky just seems to crack wide open and pour down violently. I remember that well, the sight of those huge drops pounding the windshield of our old Impala, the feeling of becoming completely drenched the moment we stepped out of the vehicle. So drenched, in fact, that moments later we could hardly feel the rain, that feeling that can only be experienced through complete immersion.

Russ had assured us that no one would be there. After all, the house had been abandoned for years and we'd have the place to ourselves. The bones of the old place had some charm, but it wasn't livable, and it would have taken lots of work and considerable resources to fix it up. But it had a roof, with a few holes mind you, but a roof, nonetheless. The floorboards were shabby, and the walls were damp even when it wasn't raining, but it was still the semblance of an edifice. It was also far enough from the center of town that it was just about completely ignored by the local police department. And unless they were called out there for something of great importance, the local officers were pretty willing to turn the other cheek regarding harmless trespassers like us.

It was just the three of us. It was always just the three of us. I had known Danny and Russ since we were in elementary school. We had run around the neighborhood together as kids when we didn't have a care in the world, when there really were no bad days and the worst thing that could happen to you was to get caught stealing candy at the general store. Those are the years when you can form a bond, a real bond, that is based on the kind of trust that can't ever be completely earned later in life. That's the type of bond I had with Danny and Russ, and we never had to think about whether we had each other's backs. It was a given, in some ways taken for granted, in other ways cherished.

Russ had been to the house before, when he and his girlfriend would steal off in the night away from parents in search of a little privacy. The house would never have been considered romantic, but when you are in high school, romance is defined differently and there is an allure that comes with the forbidden, the hidden, and the feeling of freedom that only comes from being in a place you aren't supposed to be. But Russ had been there, a few times with his girlfriend, Sheila, and they had never seen anyone. We figured if he had taken Sheila there, it must have been safe enough. And so, we followed Russ into the house.

The side door was ajar, and we entered without any problem. When we got inside, we were surprised to see how big the house was. We could see the dimensions from the outside, but we couldn't have imagined the grand, sweeping wooden staircase or the intricate pathways, back stairs, and pocket rooms that were common in old colonial homes. It was easy to see that it would have been absolutely spectacular in its day and, even now, there were elements that stood out. But it had been abandoned for so many years, and we had no idea who owned it now or if the city had simply repossessed it and let it sit due to the cost of trying to fix it up. It was the kind of place that might even have found its way onto a historic registry if it was in impeccable condition, but that would take millions of dollars and was never going to happen.

Inside the house, we all got a bit of cover from the rain, although in many areas the rain was falling into the house due to holes in the roof, which needed to be replaced. The thunder outside was violent and loud and the streaks of lightning lit up the sky. I wouldn't go as far as to say we were safe from the elements inside, but we felt slightly better being inside than outside in the rain with the electric flashes overhead.

Russ led us up the back stairs that were in pretty decent shape and down a hallway to what was clearly once a small study or library. The bookshelves even still had some moldy texts and there were a couple of couches to sit on that were actually pretty nice. It was amazing they hadn't been removed, but they were on the second floor, and that wouldn't have been an easy undertaking. In any case, we sat down and sunk into the leather as Russ tossed each of us a beer and the night cascaded down around the house.

It felt good to be sitting there with Russ and Danny, drinking beer on an old sofa, telling stories and talking about girls. Danny had a crush on Lana, but he was too nervous to talk to her. Russ said that was probably good, since she was way out of his league, and Danny did little to disagree. We all laughed and drank beer as the storm raged on. None of us were really drinkers, but it felt good to be drinking beers in the old mansion, during a storm, sitting on a couch like real men. Although we were underage, we could just as easily have been ten years older, talking about our wives or families or growing up here. There was something so completely natural about it. We'd been waiting to feel like men for a long time and, for the first time, we did.

We also felt a sense of freedom that we had never experienced. We were doing what we wanted, making our own decisions, without consequences—or at least serious ones. We drank those beers slowly, almost carefully, still getting used to the acquired taste of alcohol, with the rain outside and the feeling that we might live forever. In reality, none of us had lost our innocence. We had yet to experience the type of event that would shatter our perceptions until that night.

We had been there over an hour when we heard the creaky side door downstairs and what sounded like people stumbling into the house. "You said nobody would be here!" I exclaimed in a whisper to Russ. He looked at me with total surprise, and I could tell he was as startled as

Danny and me that someone else had entered the house. None of us dared to raise our voices or say a word. Somehow, we all knew that, if someone else was in the house, in the midst of this terrible storm, it was likely that they weren't there for anything good. We tried to be as quiet as possible. Nobody moved an inch for a couple of minutes.

Even though we were upstairs, we could hear two voices echo through the house. One of them was particularly angry, and we could hear them engaged in what sounded like a pretty unpleasant disagreement. It didn't take long for us to recognize them, and we quietly walked down the hall to see if we could get a look without being spotted.

Billy Royle was a local boy, and he was a war hero. After graduating from high school as a star athlete, he had become a member of the US Army Rangers Division. He had fought in Desert Storm, and he had returned home decorated for his actions in combat. He had received the hero's welcome he deserved, and everyone in the town took pride in his accomplishments. We lived in a small town, and someone like Billy Royle could do a lot to instill a sense of pride in people. It was the type of pride that could have a real impact, that could carry them through the dullness of their mundane lives. People who didn't have much. People who needed someone like him to believe their town was important, that they were important, and in the most extreme instances, that our time on earth counted for something.

Billy was about six years older than we were, and we didn't know him all that well. But we knew who he was. Everyone knew who he was. He had lots of job offers when he returned, but he chose to take a job working in construction. He said he couldn't see himself sitting behind a desk, and he liked working outside, feeling the elements, and continuing to utilize his considerable physical gifts. But he also planned on getting his contractor's license, and nobody doubted he would be a success.

The other voice we heard belonged to Wesley Adams. They were arguing to be sure, and Billy was angry. Wesley came from one of the wealthiest families in town, and he had never done anything of note in his life. Not until recently that is, when he realized he could get his hands on drugs that others couldn't. He had the money, and he had the connections, and he started dealing drugs before he finished high school. He had some cushy job with his father's company that he would inherit one day, but anyone in the know was aware that Wesley was dealing. Nobody gave a shit about him living off his daddy's money, but he got people's attention when he became the guy to go to if you wanted to buy drugs. In some warped way, this was the first thing Wesley had ever done to garner his own respect, even if it was criminal behavior that earned it for him.

Wesley was a senior when we were freshmen in high school. None of us did drugs, and we didn't know Wesley well either, but we knew him enough to say, "What's up, Wesley?" and it was in his best interest to know everybody. That was his job, after all, and he was always trying to make new connections that might be interested in doing business with him.

The rain seemed to be letting up just a touch. It was still coming down, but we could hear the conversation below, and we could see the back of Billy's jacket in the front hall down below the staircase without them seeing us.

"I thought you were interested in buying," said Wesley nervously and somewhat frustrated.

"No, you little shit," said Billy. "I just knew that was the way to get you to meet me here."

"Then what the fuck, Billy?"

"How could you get her hooked on that shit?" said Billy.

"Hey," said Wesley already protesting his innocence, "I just serve the customers. Nothing more. Nothing less."

"Bullshit," said Billy. "You push it and get people hooked on that shit. You fuck up their lives."

"Sorry, don't think so," said Wesley. "They do that all by themselves."

"And you knew she was alone," said Billy. "You knew I was away, that we had plans," he said, this time shoving him in the chest.

"Hey, man," chill out. "I don't get involved in that stuff."

"The fuck you don't! You are involved. You've seen her, you piece of shit. You're responsible, and it ends tonight. You are done selling that shit. You are done fucking people's lives up. Retirement is your only option."

"Billy, I'm sorry, man, but that's not how it works. I am not closing up shop because the local hero wants me to, because the town do-gooder tells me to do the right thing."

"The fuck you aren't," said Billy, shouting now. "You are done dealing, at least in this town. And if I catch you again, I will retire you myself."

"No disrespect, Billy, but this isn't Desert Storm," said Wesley with the type of arrogance you can only summon from a real sense of entitlement.

Suddenly, Billy had pulled out a gun and was pointing it at Wesley. It was clear Wesley didn't take Billy's attempt to intimidate him seriously, and we had to admit that Wesley had balls. Either that or he was completely naive. He was a spoiled, rich lowlife, but he acted like he was untouchable.

"Fuck off, Billy," said Wesley. "You aren't going to use that. I'm leaving."

Wesley took one step toward Billy and the door, and Billy just unloaded the slugs into his chest, one after the other, right there, before our eyes, at close range. Danny took the Lord's name in vain and yelled, "Jesus," if only due to shock and instinct and Billy turned to find the three of us there. He pointed his gun in our direction and said, "What the fuck are you little punks doing here?"

"We were just, just … drinking beer," Russ stammered nervously. "That's all."

Billy still had the gun pointed in our direction, with Wesley lying on the floor nearly at his feet, clearly dead from the multiple gunshots Billy embedded in him. Billy's face looked different. His eyes were vacant and terrifying, like something had snapped inside of him and he had transformed. He knew us, or at least who we were, but now he seemed to gaze upon us coldly, like strangers or worse, the enemy, simply another obstacle, and it seemed like he was contemplating the best way to handle the situation.

Danny could see that something had switched off in Billy, and he was nervous as to what he might do with that gun that was still pointed in our direction. Russ seemed to be done speaking, and I couldn't even move, my feet welded to the floor inside my boots. "Billy, you know us," said Danny, summoning the courage to speak. "We won't say nothing. Honest." Billy looked at him suspiciously, almost as if he thought we might be trying to dupe him, before Danny added, "Wesley was a bad guy"—which wasn't an endorsement of Billy's actions but not necessarily a terrible condemnation. Billy paced back and forth a little in a small space, waving the gun in frustration. He was pissed, not so much for what went down with Wesley it seemed, but rather for the unforeseen, unfortunate coincidence that we had been there to witness it. He was hopped up on adrenaline and sweating when he turned the gun back upon us.

"This is how it's gonna play out," he said emphatically. He was speaking with more confidence now, calmer, something more like what I imagined from a trained soldier in the middle of a battle. He spoke with both perfect clarity and a healthy dose of instilled fear.

"First, none of you were ever here," he said. "You didn't see a thing, and if I ever hear a word about what happened tonight—" He stopped his words, just looking at us cold and calculating and menacing.

He didn't have to say more, but I have never recovered from hearing the words exit from his mouth. "If this gets out, I will make you disappear, and I promise that you will all go down for the dirt nap if anyone breathes a word of what you have seen. But I need an insurance policy, so you are going to help me get rid of the body just so I can be sure you'll keep your mouths shut."

* * *

After that night, things were never the same with Russ, Danny, and me. They could never be the same, no matter what other forces entered or departed from our lives. We knew the right thing to do, and we didn't do it.

We were kids, after all, and we were scared, but we still knew. We knew, but we made a pact that self-preservation would have to come before moral sanctity. We put fear before justice, and we sacrificed the values and morals we had been taught to save our skin. It might have been understandable, but we all knew it was wrong. And we knew we would never recover, at least not completely. Witnessing what we did was bad enough, but disposing of the body and keeping the secret made us morally complicit.

Just the same, we graduated from high school a few months later. Danny and Russ went to college out of state and never looked back. It was as if they wanted to forget everything that had happened, everything they had seen. And decades of friendship were forced to give way. Russ settled in Colorado, where he owned a small outdoor sports store and Danny and his family lived in Minneapolis, where Danny was a successful accountant. They rarely came home to visit, only ducking in and out on the odd holiday, and they didn't attend our high school reunions. We exchanged Christmas cards, but that was about it.

I stayed in state for college. It was more affordable, and there were some good schools here. My parents didn't have the money to send me away, but I was appreciative of any opportunity to continue my education. However, it was more than that. I liked the South, the way a Southern rain poured down and the manner in which lightning cascaded across the open skies with the air still warm and moist. After college, I returned home and worked for a small accounting firm. I knew people here, and I liked it here. It was home. It would always be home.

But there were costs. I was damaged, and I knew it. I didn't get married, but that was OK. My parents hoped I would find someone and start a family, but I was never going to do that. Wesley's death had left me with a secret, a great big secret, and I carried it everywhere. It was a heavy burden, especially in a small town, and sharing my life would have meant sharing the secret. I wasn't willing to do that. So, I lived with it, with the memories, and the nightmares that always ended with the sight of Wesley's inert body full of lead. All these years later, they hadn't gone away, and it wasn't uncommon for me to wake up in a cold sweat with pictures in my mind as vivid as if it had happened yesterday.

For Billy, it was like nothing ever happened. His star was on the rise, and he began working with local politicians when he was still in the construction business.

It wasn't long before he tried the political game himself. He served as a councilman before the town elected him unanimously as our mayor, where one of his first orders of business, ironically, was the restoration of the old mansion. Just as we might have imagined, the renovated landmark eventually earned status on a historic registry, and it was something the whole town could be proud of now that it was finished.

Not surprisingly, they never found Wesley's body. Although we knew where we had disposed of it, as far as the public was concerned, it was gone without a trace. He was gone, and his parents grieved and grieved and wondered. I would see them around town, and it was easy to see they were broken, eternally broken. They offered a handsome reward to anyone who came forward with details of his disappearance or whereabouts. After a number of years, they had given up any hope of finding him alive, but they still yearned to locate his body. They still craved some form of closure.

For the parents of lost children, there is something about knowing where the body of their child is that matters, that provides closure and a sense of tragic comfort, even when life has left it. Ironically, it's not that different from the despair parents of soldiers feel when bodies disappear in foreign countries and are not able to be recovered and brought home.

I drove by Wesley's parents' house nearly every day on my way to and from work. It was a gracious home, an estate really, on the main boulevard, and I often considered stopping in to see his parents. I imagined knocking on the door, sitting down in their living room, and telling them the truth about their son. I wanted to give them the comfort of knowing what happened, but each time I decided against it—not so much motivated anymore by my own self-preservation as theirs. Wesley hadn't died with honor. He was dealing drugs, and he had been gunned down like a dog while mouthing off. It didn't exactly seem like justice, but I had a hard time believing the truth would have brought anything positive. It would have destroyed whatever precious memories they held dear, but then again it seemed they had a right to know, and who was I to conceal it from them.

Was I trying to unload this dark secret from my own troubled conscience or provide relief to theirs? Was I thinking about this as a selfish act or a truly unselfish one? Over the years, it had become hard to tell. But the memory of that night hadn't faded. In some way, it had grown stronger, more terrifying, like something I had pushed away only to see it rear its angry head again and again and again. When I woke in the night, it was nearly always to the sound of those gunshots. They had been so loud, so violent, and delivered at such close range. The sheer force. The savagery. The sound of Wesley's body colliding with the floor, almost a relief from the ferocious sound of the clip Billy had emptied. The instant manner in which the body changed, the metamorphosis as life left it. And the sheer weight of Wesley's body when Billy made us carry him out of the house. We went from kids stealing off for a beer to aging exponentially in a matter of minutes. That hadn't changed, and I remained a prisoner of that night's experience decades later. It stayed with me. The best I could do was try and distract myself and divert my thoughts when I had the chance.

It's funny how one day you can wake up and your greatest fear can be gone. It can just disappear. There is a tipping point, when the facade becomes so torturous that the fear no longer appears suffocating. It no longer seems terrifying. And that's how I felt when I woke up that morning surer than I had ever been about anything in my life. Surer about what I had to do, what I wanted to do, what I was going to do. Even before I had done it, I felt unburdened. It felt good, and I knew I would never have to feel the impossible weight of that guilt again.

I pulled my feet to the edge of the bed, wiped my face with my dry hands and made my way to the shower. I took the time to shave, combed my hair neatly, and grabbed a flannel shirt and jeans that looked casual but still nice. I walked into the kitchen to grab a muffin and a cup of coffee but, truth be told, I couldn't get out of there fast enough. It was as if I was now running toward something that I had been running from for years. I can't really explain it, except to say that I was moving with unwavering certainty.

When I pulled up to the Adams' estate, it looked exactly the same as it always had. The landscaping hadn't changed from the time we'd been in high school, every hedge and manicured lawn cut just the same as I remembered. The windows were original and only the shutters had been painted. There had been no additions, and the external dimensions of the house remained identical to the original design. Time stood still here, the past and the present seemingly interchangeable, if only on the surface. But I was there, after all this time, to confirm their worst fears, the worst fears any parent can have. I was there to tell them that their son Wesley was dead.

It was still morning. The air was crisp. I parked on the smooth, oval driveway, stepped out of my car into the bright sunlight, and walked to the door.

I WOULDN'T HAVE KNOWN

I wouldn't have known the barbershop was open on Sundays if I hadn't skipped church that morning. But I was tired of sermons. I got them at school. I got them at home. And on the weekends, I got them at church.

My father didn't love church, but he respected it. His father had been a preacher, and so it was pretty much ingrained in him that he was going to be a man of faith. He didn't have much of a choice, and he obliged. It seemed he always obliged.

Mom was different. She counted on the church, needed the church, almost yearned for it. Sunday mornings couldn't come fast enough for her. The other six days were simply a warm-up, a precursor to the main event where she did everything she could to be a good Catholic, to live by the stringent guidelines of her faith, and then be rewarded for it inside the holy building on Sunday. It meant so much to her that she often laid out her outfit two days before.

My brother and I were expected to do the same. My brother always did it dutifully, if not enthusiastically. But he accepted it. And he didn't question it. This meant wearing dress clothes that were perfectly pressed, each and every Sunday. It meant laying them out beforehand, so that Mom could see them, inspect them, and approve of them. And it meant being good Catholics and being on our best behavior, ideally, all of the time.

I was a harder case. I didn't like wearing dress clothes. Moreover, I didn't see why we had to wear dress clothes. They were hot, itchy. And the collar always felt like it was choking the life out of me. I wasn't afraid to voice my opinion, and I told my mother exactly how I felt. I spoke to her direct and clear and purposeful, even if it seemed to go against the Church. I wasn't drawn to Catholicism, and truth be told, I didn't see why I had to be. It seemed like a sham.

"You don't really mean that," she'd say.

But I absolutely did mean that. I meant everything I said about the Church—from the attire to the sermons. But the sermons were the worst, the absolute worst. They just seemed so phony and far-fetched to me. Hearing a man up there, a mortal man, as mortal as I was, speaking about God. It just didn't play well. It never played well, not with me. Then we had to take communion and drink the "Blood of Christ" out of a silver goblet. The hypocrisy of it all. Dying for our sins. Yeah, sure. That's just what he was thinking. I never bought it, not for a minute, and I told my mother that. But she just shook her head, upset but patient, and said, "One day you'll understand."

My dad was just along for the ride. I never believed for a minute that he bought into the Church, but he wouldn't have dared let Mom know this. He wouldn't have considered challenging her. He really was the perfect churchgoing husband. Always on time. Always dressed well. And without any hint of rebellion. Still, I could tell his heart wasn't in it. That it was never really in it. But he was dutiful above all. If I were venturing to guess, I would have said he was more dutiful to my mother than to the Church. To my mother, they were one and the same.

She told us this in no uncertain terms. "If you respect me," she said emphatically, "then you'll respect the Church."

Although she really believed this, we just saw it as a clever way to guilt us into showing respect for an institution that held far less value for us than for her. To some degree, her tactic worked. My dad and my brother were basically altar boys, and I went to church more times in my youth than I ever would have, had my mother not guilted me into it.

* * *

I had told my parents I was going to sleep over at Tommy Wilson's house on Saturday night. They said that was alright, so long as I made it to church the next morning. Tommy's house was just around the corner from church anyway, and his family went to Sunday morning Mass every week as well. My parents had no problem with me staying over at Tommy's, so I packed a bag and took my dress clothes with me.

What they didn't know is I had no plans to go to Tommy Wilson's house. At least not on Saturday. Not on this Saturday. My girlfriend Melissa's parents were out of town, and we were planning to spend the night together. We had never spent a night together before, and this was going to be the first time. It was the first time for both of us. I tried not to let on to Melissa, but I was nervous. I hoped she was nervous too. At least a little.

Melissa had been my girlfriend for all four years of high school. She was smart, damn smart, and much smarter than I was. I wasn't dumb, but I wouldn't say I applied myself. In fact, I did the bare minimum to get by. Melissa was just the opposite. She was smart, did the best that she could in every class, and was rewarded for it. She was going to study at an Ivy League school in the fall, while I wasn't even sure I was going to college.

This made me wonder why she would want to go out with a guy like me, but I tried not to question it for fear that I might jinx it. I tried not to doubt it, and it wasn't so different from my mother's blind faith in the Church. But I liked her. I really liked Melissa. I liked her a lot.

When I got to her house that night, I was carrying my bags. I had brought a small overnight bag, along with a hanging bag that included my dress clothes for church the next day that Mom had approved when she thought I was going over to Tommy Wilson's house.

"You can put your bags in my room," said Melissa.

I carried my bags up the stairs and set them down in the corner of Melissa's room. Her bed was made neatly, and it had lots of pillows on it along with a couple of stuffed animals that reminded me we were still kids in many ways. Melissa followed me up the stairs and kissed me after I put my bags down. We had discussed her parents going out of town beforehand, and we were both excited and a little scared to be together, alone together, for the first time. I tried not to let on, but I was shaking a little until Melissa realized and had an idea.

"Let's order pizza!" said Melissa, in part I think because it was dinnertime, but also to break the awkwardness of our being alone in her house together.

"OK," I said.

So, we ordered a large cheese pizza with soda and watched a movie in the small den off the living room in her house. We sat together on the sofa, and she leaned into me sweetly while I stroked her hair. When the movie ended, we just sat in the dark, the sound of our breathing all we could hear with our hearts racing and not knowing exactly what to do.

"Come on," Melissa said, smiling. "Let's go upstairs."

We walked upstairs holding hands, and then I sat on the bed while Melissa went to the bathroom. I went to the bathroom when she came out. In the bathroom, I brushed my teeth and just stared at the mirror full of doubt. Every doubt you could have in the world it seemed. Was I good-looking enough? Was I smart enough? Would I be good enough? The longer I looked, the more I questioned myself. Finally, I turned away and opened the door to find Melissa underneath her white sheets with her clothes in a pile on the side of the bed. She was smiling. Even when she was nervous, she was smiling. She was always smiling.

I undressed shyly and climbed into bed where we fumbled around clumsily and did our best to take care of one another lovingly and respectfully. When it was over Melissa made me feel like the best guy in the world, even if I was an amateur by any standard. I tried to make her feel equally cherished, and once the shock and awe had worn off for both of us, we were laughing again, this time more naturally, entwined together beneath the sheets in one another's arms. She leaned into me, and I stroked her hair just as I had done on the sofa.

We woke up the next morning with the sun streaming in through Melissa's upstairs window that faced the backyard. She looked beautiful, with her hair falling imperfectly around her face and her smile welcoming me to a new day for the first time. It only took me one second to determine that I was not going to church that Sunday.

My mother wasn't all that supportive of my relationship with Melissa. She liked Melissa. There wasn't much not to like, but Melissa wasn't Catholic, and that meant a lot to my mother. It only seemed fitting that I miss church after what would undoubtedly have been viewed as a night of sin in my mother's eyes. But the truth was I wanted to be with Melissa. We had shared something special, earthly delights that seemed as close as I was ever going to get to heaven anyway.

"I'm starving," said Melissa. "Let's go out and get something to eat."

She always knew just how to lighten the mood, and she often did so by suggesting we get something to eat. She knew I never turned down food, and she always knew the right time to suggest we seek it out.

"That sounds great," I said. "I am hungry too."

We went to an old breakfast spot in a part of town that had largely been forgotten in the era of new strip malls and chain restaurants. But it had been there forever, and they made the best breakfast burritos in town, maybe anywhere for that matter. We sat down at a table in the corner. One thing for sure was that none of my mom's friends were going to see us there, since they were all at church.

We mowed the food down quickly. I wasn't sure if we were starving or if it was just residual nervous energy from the night before. Either way, we ate like we were famished. Like we'd never eaten before. I liked that Melissa wasn't afraid to eat when she was hungry. Other girls rarely ate on dates, but Melissa wasn't like that. The food tasted better than ever. I paid the bill, and we walked out feeling very satisfied. The bell on the door jingled as it closed gently behind us.

We didn't have any plans until Melissa spotted an old-school barbershop a couple of doors down. "That's where I got my first haircut," I said. "My dad's been taking me there ever since. The barber Vince is a great guy."

"Let's go get you a haircut now," said Melissa excitedly. "Will you let me tell him exactly how I want them to style it?"

"Sure," I said without hesitating.

I would have said anything at that moment. I was with Melissa. We had shared the best night of my life. And I was missing church.

We walked in, and there was nobody waiting. Vince turned when he heard the door, and he immediately looked surprised to see me. He looked at Melissa and seemed to have an idea of what was going on.

"Aren't you supposed to be in church?" he asked, smiling.

I smiled back without saying a word and said, "Vince, this is my girlfriend, Melissa."

"Nice to meet you, Melissa," said Vince. "I've known this kid a long time."

"That's what he told me," said Melissa. "Nice to meet you too."

"So, what are we gonna do today?" asked Vince. "The usual?"

"Not sure," I said. "Melissa's calling the shots today."

"That's how it starts, my boy," said Vince, laughing. "You're a brave man. I've been married twenty-seven years, and I still won't let my wife tell anyone how to cut my hair. This must be love."

Melissa and I looked at each other and started laughing. It was nice not to be in church, and it was nice to be there with her, talking to Vince and getting my haircut. Melissa then whispered instructions in Vince's ear, and Vince raised his eyebrows to make me nervous. But they were just messing with me, and the haircut was actually pretty normal, except she just left it a little longer on top. But nothing too special. I paid Vince and said thanks before he stopped me.

"I assume your folks don't know about you being here with Melissa?" he said.

"No, they don't," I replied. "I'd like to keep it that way. Mom would be furious if she knew I was here. I'm sure I'm going to catch hell anyway for missing church."

"Catch hell. I like that," said Vince. "Well, your secret's safe with me. Speaking of church, though, is Jimmy McIntyre still the priest over there?"

"Oh yeah," I said. "Father McIntyre is still there. I didn't even know he had a first name."

"Probably shouldn't tell you this, but since I am keeping a secret for you, I've got one for you."

"Alright," I said.

Melissa was right by my side. She was feeling my head with her hands and seemed to like the new haircut.

"You know I went to high school with your parents?" said Vince. "Overlapped with them for one year."

"Yeah, I think I knew that," I said.

"Well, Jimmy McIntyre was a senior in college when your parents were seniors in high school, and he dated your mom. This was long before she got together with your dad, and not many people knew about it. Pretty sure your dad didn't know about it either. I only know because Jimmy is just a year older than me, and we were friends in high school. He was pretty head over heels for your mom, but ultimately her parents were against it. Thought she was too young, and he was too wild. Not long after your mom broke it off, he joined the seminary.

"Holy shit," said Melissa.

I had never heard her swear before. Not ever.

"Why are you telling me this?" I asked.

"Well, because I know you are a good kid. You've always been a good kid, and I have always liked you. Now that I've met Melissa, I like her too. By the way, you should definitely keep her around," he whispered in my ear loud enough to make sure Melissa could hear, and she smiled.

"I like her too," I said, overstating the obvious.

"Plus," said Vince, "I know you are going to catch hell, holy hell, for missing church today, and I figured you deserved to have some ammunition to use in return when you get home. Seems only fair."

"Thanks, Vince," I said. "Thank you."

I looked at Melissa, and she still had a look of disbelief. I was dumbfounded too. My mom and Father McIntyre. It seemed so implausible. My mind was racing. Was it the Church she was devoted to or did she just like listening to her ex-boyfriend every Sunday morning? What if she had never gotten over him? What if? I didn't even want to let it cross my mind. It was almost too much to comprehend.

"This is quite a revelation," said Melissa.

"It would be," I said, "if we weren't talking about my mother."

Melissa and I walked back to her parents' house and sat on the sofa. We didn't say much until she kissed me and told me she loved me. I told her I loved her too, even if I was too scared to say it first. She was so much braver than I was, and she made me feel strong. She made me feel like I was worth something, something real, something more real than going to church and worshipping God, if God even existed, spun through the words of my mom's ex-boyfriend.

It was time to go home, and I stood up and walked to the door. I kissed Melissa like a man who was going off to war. I kissed her with my whole heart, and I held her head in my hands as she kissed me back. I walked out the door and heard her say, "Good luck."

When I walked into our house, my mother was sitting in the kitchen. She was still in her clothes from church, and my dad was upstairs in his office. I stood tall, while she shook her head in disgust and her eyes burned a hole in me. It was all so condescending, and now it seemed hypocritical too. It seemed like such a sham, and the scorn I felt only made me want to reveal what Vince had shared with us at the barbershop.

But I also saw my mom as human, more human, perhaps truly human, for the first time. She wasn't really holier than thou, now that her own morality had been unveiled. Instead of looking at her with bitterness and anger, I almost felt a touch of sadness. Maybe not sadness, but I think I understood her more than ever before. I understood her, and in some strange way, I felt close to her. I no longer wanted to hurt her or get back at her or break her heart. I wasn't even sure I wanted to resist her anymore.

"I'm so disappointed in you," she said, still sitting down in a chair at the kitchen table.

"I ... I'm sorry," I replied. "I know you are disappointed, and I am sorry."

"Thank you," she said. "Thank you for saying that. Why don't we go ahead and set those clothes out for next Sunday?"

THE CLOTHES

After my mother died, there was so much to do. That might sound cold, but if it's cold, then it is the cold, harsh reality. And, to be perfectly honest, it's the reality of what it takes to bury the dead. It takes a lot to bury the dead, and it takes more when you're the oldest, the oldest of four brothers. It's a lonesome climb. I'm sorry if this sounds like I'm complaining when, after all, I wasn't the one who died. But it's a lot, a whole heck of a lot.

Make no mistake, the living are given a list, a task list, and it's no small thing. Perhaps this task list was initially created with good intentions—little more than a ploy, a ruse, to get us to turn our attention to something, anything, other than the death that has just occurred. If, in fact, this is the rationale behind the list, then I can appreciate it to a degree, or at the very least say that it did go quite a long way to diverting my attention in the aftermath.

Because, when my mom died, I was busy, real busy. I had no idea how busy I'd be, but I was busy. There were just so many things I'd never considered. There were authorities to be contacted so the body could be removed. There was the urgent need to compose an obituary and then make sure it was delivered to the appropriate media outlets. Since my mother had selected a burial, a casket had to be purchased, and there were more options than I could count. It was unreal. You can send someone down into the earth in a Rolls Royce or a Chevrolet. No joke. I promise you there are more considerations than you ever imagined. After that was sorted, as if that wasn't enough, I spent hours on the phone. Death certificates. Credit card cancellations. Online registrations. Insurance companies. And then, without much time, we had to prepare. After all, we'd be entertaining in the form of a funeral, followed by receiving people at our home. In reality, it's not all that different from the work of planning a wedding, other than the fact that it's a sad occasion and it has to be planned in a period of twenty-four hours.

You might be wondering about my father, and this isn't meant to disparage him at all. Not in any way. Not ever. But when my mother died, my father couldn't help, not really anyway. And I couldn't ask for his help. I just couldn't. He was in a trance, a real trance, not just a numbness, but more like a stupor. It almost seemed like he failed to comprehend what had actually happened, the sheer disbelief of it, and he was paralyzed psychologically. Of course, he knew, but something about the surreal nature of the situation failed to register. It was just as well. Plus, he had my brothers, my younger brothers, and that was all he could handle and more. At times like this, younger brothers don't want their big brother. They want what they've lost, and that's a parent. So, I just went on knocking out tasks, doing what had to be done without apology. Forgive the term, but it's a blood sport, and only the cold-hearted survive. In some ways, it wasn't so different from the manner my mom had deployed in order to run our family so efficiently. Tasks upon tasks upon tasks with little help. Far too little help. If she had stopped for a moment to contemplate the scope, she'd have surely collapsed. But she just kept going, and that's what I did.

If it sounds like I haven't appropriately conveyed any real emotion here, that's probably because I haven't. But that's what a death in the family does to you. It doesn't allow you the time to feel, really feel the impact of what has occurred. It doesn't provide you with the appropriate opportunity to honor the person you've lost through the genuine emotion you have inside. Mourning, quite frankly, is a luxury few have on the heels of death. And while this might help you survive the initial days following a life's expiration, it will not prepare you to live however many days lay ahead.

That's what happened to me when my mother died. I got right down to business, stepped up and took a leadership role in the family—managed each task with the calm of a veteran businessman in a corporate board meeting. I was steely, poised, and seemingly unflappable. When droves of people descended upon our home, I was gracious. It was as if I was playing a role, a role I was born to play, with relative ease. I was making the impossible look easy and effortless to the dismay of the masses. And then, nearly as quickly as they had appeared, they were gone. All of them. The people. Just gone. All of them, as if they had vanished, returned to their lives and families and jobs. Their days piled up in front of them just like the days before, a stark reminder that the world just keeps going, turning, on and on and on, with or without you.

Meanwhile, the glare of the lights had now faded for me. The house was now filled with only our voices, and I was exhausted, as if all of the energy had drained from my body, permanently. My dad helped my brothers return to their lives—going back to school, playing sports, and interacting with friends. But I didn't have the motivation to do anything, not anymore, and getting out of bed to make it to the refrigerator felt like more energy than I was willing to expend. Furthermore, it was now, and only now, that the house revealed what it had lost—not only my mother's energy, but the external forces that had filled it in the days prior, when our front hall had been filled with people offering their condolences. Even the days leading up to her death were, in a way, lively. Our extended family all around. Caregivers coming and going. The doctor stopping by. Everyone still participating in something of a hustle, a dance, a choreographed scene that was playing out. Now, it just felt like everything, not just my mother's life, but everything in the world, in my world, was over. In the wake of these changes, I had gone from being a fully functioning robot to being terribly depressed.

It was conceivable that I might stay in bed for months but, ultimately, there were other things to do. Things that weren't time-sensitive like those immediate tasks in the hours following her death, but things that were still important, that had to be done. One of these items on our list was what to do with my mother's clothes. Since she was the only woman in the house, none of us could use them. And there were so many clothes, so many clothes left over. Furthermore, my dad didn't want them sitting in his closet forever. It was just too hard, too hard for him to walk in there and see her blouses and dresses and slacks and shoes lined up the way they had always been. He simply couldn't face that thought every time he changed his own clothes, and so he asked me to find a good place for us to donate them.

Not knowing where to start, I decided to look through my mother's book of telephone numbers. We had donated clothes before, when our clothes got too small or too old or we simply didn't like a particular style anymore. This was, of course, my mother's idea. My mother had impressed upon us from a young age that, if we weren't going to wear the clothes, there was always someone out there who would be grateful to have them. The worst thing we could do was let clothes sit and go to waste, and she refused to let this happen.

Her book of phone numbers and addresses was inside the top drawer of her small desk in the kitchen. There was a corded phone on top of the desk, and my mother spent countless hours there, paying the bills, coordinating schedules, and making phone calls the way we used to make them, before cellular phones let us roam unrestricted. The desk was representative of the unimaginable amount of time my mother spent running our family, and the book was filled with names and numbers, addresses, calendars, and notes in the margins. It was the most utilitarian book, and yet the outside was lovely, with a pattern of flowers on the cover that was delicate and colorful. Flowers, that grow from the earth, that turn into something beautiful. Flowers on the outside, so full and in bloom, covering a dead woman's book of life's important details.

I hadn't expected the book to get to me, not when I had already been through so much without flinching, but there was something about it that struck the most painful blow. Something different, more revealing, more personal. Her handwriting. Nothing, no nothing, had bothered me so much as seeing my mother's handwriting, her distinct crafting of the alphabet's letters, her shorthand, the construction of words and thoughts authored by her and her alone. Few things about a person speak so loudly without saying a word. Handwriting tells so much about a person, and the sight of it allowed me to hear my mother's voice for the first time since she had died. It was then, and only then, that I was overcome by the emotion I felt realizing I would never hear her voice again, that it had been silenced for eternity, trapped below the surface, accessible only through memory. The tears begin to well up in the large basins of my eyes and stream down my face. I wasn't sure I would ever be able to stop them.

The next morning, I returned to her desk. I was ready this time, and I sat down in her chair and pulled out the book. I dialed up the number of the store and spoke to a very nice man. He was used to receiving these kinds of calls when people died even if I wasn't used to making them. But he had just the right tone, and he put me at ease. He made me feel as if I was doing the right thing, as if my mother would feel I was doing the right thing, and he did it without overstepping his boundaries. He just made me feel good, and I felt good, genuinely good, for the first time in months. I didn't know why, but I felt good. I had stared at her handwriting, and I had made the phone call. It wasn't until I heard his voice that I knew I would be alright, that I knew, eventually, everything would be alright. Although I had lost my mother's voice, it seemed as if I had found mine again.

I was grateful for that, and I was grateful to him. On the phone, I cleared my throat like a much older man, and I arranged a time for us to come by and donate my mother's clothes.

WIDOWERS

They were old men, two old men, and they met for breakfast every Thursday morning. They had been meeting the same place for years, long before either of them was married. As kids, they would go to eat there with their families nearly every Saturday morning. It was just a delicatessen. But it was their delicatessen, in their hometown, filled with their town's people. And this made the deli a special place. It was a special place, and they still liked to go there. They still liked to go there every week, and they never missed. So many things in their lives had moved through the terrifying windows of time. But the delicatessen remained, just as it always had, almost as if it was waiting for them.

Each man had been married for a long time, but they were now widowers. Al had been married for forty-six years before his wife died over a decade ago. Dennis had lost his wife more recently, just last year, when she succumbed to cancer after a six-year battle. Dennis and his wife had enjoyed fifty-seven years of marriage.

The old men knew they were lucky. They knew this, and they felt this. They understood it was a blessing to have loved so strong. To have loved so long. They were grateful they had children and grandchildren. They would have been considered fortunate by any standard, and yet they were still widowers. And they were still men, trying to stave off the dark, navigating their final years alone.

"You never get used to it," said Al. "Her being gone. It's an ache that only grows with the years."

"I never imagined I would be alone," said Dennis.

"Me either," said Al. "Always figured I would go first."

"Life is strange," said Dennis. "Who would have thought we'd be here, just the two of us, after all these years, alone?"

"Not me," said Al. "Not ever. How are you dealing with it?"

"Not that well," said Dennis. "Do you ever get used to it?"

"Well, I am not sure," said Al. "I haven't. When I walk in that dark house each night, I still wait for her voice."

"The house holds the memories," said Dennis.

"It's true," said Al.

"I don't know what to do," confessed Dennis.

"I haven't even moved any of Sandy's things," said Al. "Twelve years and the drawers are still filled. Her clothes still hang in the closet. I have given the kids some of her jewelry, but that's about it."

Really?" said Dennis. "You never told me that."

"The kids think it's creepy. And they think seeing her things keeps me from moving on."

"Do you think that's true?" asked Dennis. "That having her things around has kept you from moving on?"

"Who says I am trying to move on?" snapped Al. "Who says you have to? Just because the days move on, doesn't mean you have to. I like seeing her things where they've always been."

"I understand. Or, at least, I think I do," said Dennis. "But it made me too sad to see all of her clothes each day.

I felt better giving them away, even if it didn't feel right. Well, perhaps not better, but it made it easier for me, not necessarily to move on, but to face the day."

"I get that too," said Al. "See you still wear your wedding ring though?"

"I do," said Dennis.

"Why do you wear yours?" asked Al, who also still wore his wedding ring after all these years.

"I guess," said Dennis, "I guess I still feel married. After all, it's not like we split up."

"I get it," said Al. "Some people give me a hard time about it, but they don't understand."

"They are probably well-intentioned," said Dennis.

"I suppose," said Al. "Mostly, though, I feel good wearing my wedding ring. I never wanted to take it off when she was alive, and I don't want to now."

"Good for you," said Dennis.

For many years, Al and Dennis had brought their families to the delicatessen. The kids loved it, especially the grilled cheese sandwiches, and their wives enjoyed seeing each other even if they could have done with a little less grease. It was a real greasy spoon, just a classic American deli, not an elegant thing in the joint, but it was a part of their lives. It had always been part of their lives.

Now, their kids were grown and had moved away. The world was changing, but the deli didn't change with the times. No website. No electronic buzzer to hold while waiting for a table. Just pen and paper. A list of names on legal pad, yellow legal pad, and a clipboard in the arms of the hostess. It was that kind of place.

"Did you hear about Zelzer?" asked Dennis.

"I did," said Al. "Was sorry to hear his wife passed away. She was a nice woman."

"Yes, she was," said Dennis. "But I wasn't talking about that. Did you hear he already moved in with Bonnie?"

"Bonnie Simpson?" asked Al. "Joe's widow?"

"Yes," said Dennis. "Heard about it this week."

"That was fast," said Al. "I'm surprised."

"I was too," said Dennis. "Only been a couple months since his wife passed away."

The men finished their meal. They finished, and they just sat there talking. There was nowhere else for them to go, and they liked to sit there talking. They each took a cup of coffee before the meal and one after. They were now on their second cups, always black—no sugar either. Strong.

"Losing your spouse is tough," said Al. "And some guys just can't be alone."

"But you've been alone," said Dennis. "You've been alone for a long time."

"I have, but that doesn't mean I like it. I'm lonely as hell. The house is dark and too big for me. I sit at my desk with my small lamp and hope the hours at night pass quicker."

"You could start dating," said Dennis.

"I said I was lonely," said Al. "I didn't say I was crazy."

"So, you don't want to date?" inquired Al.

"No."

"Do you ever think you'll date?" Al followed up.

"No."

"I am not sure I understand," said Dennis. "You're lonely, but you don't want to meet anyone else?"

"That's right," said Al. "Now you're getting it, pal."

"Sorry if I made you uncomfortable," said Dennis. "All this is new to me."

"You didn't make me uncomfortable," said Al. "I am perfectly comfortable talking about it."

"OK," said Dennis.

"I am not looking for sympathy or encouragement," said Al. "That's what everyone thinks."

"They are probably just trying to be helpful."

"It's just that I've decided that part of my life is over. That's all."

"Were there opportunities?" asked Dennis.

"Some," said Al. "Especially in the beginning. Remember when Sally wanted to set me up with Dixie Larsen?"

"Oh gosh, that's right," said Dennis. "She was a friend of Sally's, and Sally thought you two would be good together."

"I remember, Dennis," said Al. "It's fine."

The waitress came by the table to see if they wanted anything else. She knew them, and she had a pretty good understanding of when to swing by and when to give them more space. She had noticed the men had stopped talking and took the opportunity to check on them.

"Want to split a lemon meringue pie?" asked Al.

"Well, I shouldn't," hesitated Dennis.

"What do you care?" snapped Al. "Not like you're watching your figure."

"Ah, what the hell. Sure," said Dennis.

"A piece of lemon meringue pie," said Al, triumphant. "Whipped cream, and two forks please if it's not too much trouble."

"One piece of lemon meringue pie," she announced. "Coming right up, gentlemen."

It was late in the morning, and the breakfast crowd had thinned out. The working folks had hustled toward their jobs. It was nearly empty. The two men just sat there, with the sound of the fluorescent lights buzzing over their heads. Before too long, the lunch hour would be upon them. Lunch hour was a busy time at the delicatessen, and the old men liked to finish before the rush. Local businessmen and women. Twenty-somethings who slept in late. And, of course, the old ladies who came straight from the hair salons.

It was probably too early for lemon meringue pie, or at least that's what their wives would have told them. But they were widowers now. They were men who'd lost their wives, and there's only so much anyone can tell men who've lost their wives. And why would they listen anyway? They didn't have much, but they could have a piece of lemon meringue pie. And that's what they were going to do. The waitress returned and placed the pie in the center of the table. It had a large dollop of whipped cream, and there were two forks on the plate. The men nodded approvingly, as they sat in front of the large, glass window with the morning sun streaming in.

"Here you go," she said and smiled.

LEAVING TOWN

"You ever think about just hitting the road and leaving town?" I asked my wife.

We had been married for years, and we had always lived in the same town.

"You mean on a vacation?" she asked.

"No, just hitting the road. Taking off. Leaving. Packing up, getting in the car, and just heading out."

"Forever?" she asked, strangely.

"I am not sure what forever means," I said. "But permanently. Just deciding we are going to go somewhere else and live."

"Are you kidding?" asked my wife.

"Do I look like I'm kidding?" I responded with all seriousness.

"What's got into you?" she started again. "We've lived here our whole lives."

"Exactly," I said flatly.

"But we have friends here," she added, continuing to make what she thought was a very obvious case.

"We can make new friends," I replied.

She looked at me sideways, in a way she had never looked at me before. She looked at me like I was a stranger.

"New friends?" she said, quizzically. "Is there something wrong with our old friends?"

"Nothing at all," I said. "They are our friends, and they will still be our friends if we leave."

"But why would we leave?" she asked. "Our life is here."

"It doesn't have to be," I remarked. "Haven't you ever thought of living somewhere else?"

"Maybe when I was young," she said. "For a brief moment, but that was a long time ago."

Her response wasn't all that unsurprising, but it wasn't making it easier. We usually saw eye to eye. We had raised two grown kids together, and that's not easy. We had weathered recessions and the loss of parents. And we were getting to the age where friends were starting to die unexpectedly.

"What about Monty?" I asked. "Do you ever think about him, that he and Sheila never went anywhere."

"I think he had a good life," she said. "And they had a good marriage here in town. I don't think they lived with regrets."

"Do you think Monty died with them?" I countered.

"Not that I know of," she answered. "I think he was content."

"Are you content?" I asked. "Are you content if this is all there is, if this is the hand we play from here on out?"

"We are so lucky, honey," she said, trying to sweet-talk me just a tad. "We've been unbelievably fortunate to be dealt such a good hand."

"That's true," I agreed. "But the cards can change so quickly. They did for Monty."

"Is that it?" she said. "Are you worried that one day you'll just get bad news?"

"Yes," I said. "Or you will. I worry about it all the time."

"That seems like a hard way to live," she said. "Just waiting for the other shoe to drop."

"Only if you're waiting," I remarked. "That's why I don't want to wait. That's why I don't want to wait for one minute. This worry doesn't depress me so much as inspire me, inspire me to live—really live."

"And you think that means getting in a car and just driving?" she asked skeptically. "Is that your definition of living?"

"Yes, in a sense," I said. "At the very least, it's one definition of living, throwing caution to the wind when you have nothing holding you down."

"But it's not the only definition," she said, retreating to her position. "We are living well now."

"I am not in disagreement. We live well, but we have a routine. The days are predictable. We have a basic idea of what we can expect."

"Is there anything wrong with that?" she asked. "To live well and embrace the comfort of routines, friends, things we can count on."

"It's definitely a safe bet," I added.

"A safe bet doesn't necessarily mean a bad bet."

"It doesn't mean a good one either," I said. "It may be prudent, but it doesn't get your adrenaline going."

"Adrenaline? Is that what you're looking for?" she asked. "You are not twenty-five anymore. Haven't we had enough adrenaline and anxious moments raising two children and all that comes with it? Now you want to seek new thrills?"

"I am not sure I want to seek thrills," I answered, trying to be calm as she began to exhibit more and more frustration with my stubbornness. "But I want to feel my heart quicken. I want to feel it quicken like it did when we were young, when everything was new and we threw ourselves into the unknown with fearlessness."

"I don't want my heart to quicken anymore," she said. "It's been through enough. I am not brave anymore."

I recognized that this was hard for her to say. And it was hard for me to hear. She was ready to settle into our routine and remain there. In fact, she desired it, chose it, perhaps even needed it—not merely to feel good but to feel safe."

"I thought I made you feel safe," I suggested, trying to lighten the mood a little.

She smiled and said, "Well, you do, honey. You do, but you're not as young as you once were."

"Age is a state of mind," I responded, trying to ignore her sobering response.

"The mirror says something different," she answered. "And ... so does your birth certificate."

That wasn't easy to hear, but of course she was right. I was no longer a young man. My body had begun to break down a bit, and I had a soft belly where a tight stomach once sat. My back was fragile, and my arms weren't nearly as strong as they once were. But I tried not to think about those things, not because they weren't true, but rather because I couldn't really see the benefit of embracing that reality. I tried to think about all of the things I could do (or hoped to do) rather than the ones I couldn't.

"Imagine what life would be like if we didn't count the years going by," I said.

"That's a nice thought," she responded. "But I think we would know."

"How?" I asked.

"Your body would tell you," she said, as if it was an obvious deduction.

"Of course, our bodies communicate to us," I concurred. "But what if you didn't have the knowledge of an end date or an average life expectancy? You wouldn't know how close you were to it."

"Sure, you would," she remarked. "That's why some animals go off to die on their own when they know they are at the end of their lives."

"Maybe, but they also don't worry about the end until the end, until the very end, when all hope is lost. That's hardly the case for us."

She didn't say anything, choosing to pause, in part, I think, due to exhaustion. The conversation was exhausting, and I had the reputation of being able to wear just about anyone out in this regard. That was my basic approach to life. I wasn't intimidating at first glance but, in a war of attrition, I had the ability to outlast just about anyone. My wife looked into my eyes. She wasn't looking at me like I was a stranger anymore, but she was looking.

She was looking as if trying to determine how personal this was for me and how far I might be willing to take it. Although I was an open book and there were no secrets between us, my wife had the ability to see right through me, to my very soul. I could see she was peering into the greatest depths of me with those eyes that could level me from the very first time I met their gaze all those years ago. But this time she chose not to level me, despite her best instincts. She understood my vulnerability in ways nobody else did. She understood, and she sacrificed herself for me time and time again. It might have looked like I was the strong one, but the truth was she had been taking care of me for a long time when it came to my emotional needs. We were lovers and we were partners and we were friends. Even when we saw things from different perspectives, we were still friends. Best friends. And no matter how angry one of us might make the other, we could only ever imagine our life together. We could never imagine lying down in bed without the other. Of this, there was never any doubt. Furthermore, people might have seen me as easygoing, but I knew better. She was the first person with the courage to love me, love all of me, and I was only a tower of strength for as long I was breathing her air. She knew this, and she never let me down.

"Will you protect me?" she asked coyly, knowing my limitations.

"Of course," I said, pretending I was young again. "Has there ever been a doubt?"

"And if I get cold at night …," she added. "You'll promise to hold me the whole night through."

"From start to finish," I said confidently.

"We can pretend we don't know how old we are," she said. "It's what we will have to do if this is going to be a success."

"You are still young to me," I said, almost believing it.

"We've been young before," she said, with a swagger she no longer possessed. "Why should this be any different?"

She was being playful, playing along with me, but she was playing with my heart too, and in this regard, I knew her to be the gentlest creature alive. She kissed me tenderly and placed one hand on the side of my face.

"OK," she said as she stood up, slapping her thighs. "Come on, you old fool. If we are going to do this, we'd better start packing. It's important we leave at the crack of dawn and get out of town before the sun comes up. You know how I hate traffic."

ABOUT THE AUTHOR

David Joseph is the award-winning author of *The Old Men Who Row Boats and Other Stories*. His writing has been published in *The Wall Street Journal*, *LA Times*, *London Magazine*, *Doubletake Magazine*, *Motherwell*, and *Rattle*. He is a graduate of Hobart College and the University of Southern California's Graduate Writing Program, where he was a recipient of the Kerr Fellowship and served as editor for the *Southern California Anthology*. In 2002 he cofounded the nonprofit organization America SCORES LA, and in 2007 he received the John Henry Hobart Fellowship for Ethics and Social Justice. He has taught at Harvard University and Pepperdine University. In 2019 he was awarded a position on the Fulbright Specialist Roster.

Made in the USA
Las Vegas, NV
28 July 2023